MW01228626

SECRETS

SPIES, LIES & CRIMINAL TIES

ALAN FYSEN

Secrets: Spies, Lies, and Criminal Ties
© 2017 Alan Eysen

Layout and Print Book Production by Eunice Sibrian
Cover Art © Berge Design

Published by Seven Es, LLC
Distributed by Bublish, Inc.
bublish.com

ISBN-10:1-946229-50-4
ISBN-13:978-1-946229-50-2

TABLE OF CONTENTS

1

A PECULIAR DEATH

It was not so much the way he lived but the way he died that made Army Captain Albert Ruppert Manigrove III so interesting to the Jefferson County Coroner.

Manigrove's body was found off the Dixie Highway, the main link between Fort Knox and Louisville, Kentucky, 30 miles away. Initially, police thought he had been struck by a car or truck. But the coroner's office found that he was run over after he died. His outward physical injuries were postmortem.

"A heavy vehicle, probably a truck, hit him and broke a lot of his bones and organs," the coroner said, " but his blood had already pooled and all his organs were smashed to jelly. This guy wasn't road kill." The coroner also was certain the captain had not suffered a stroke or heart attack. "He was in his early 40s and in pretty good health," he told State Police Detective Sergeant Mike Theiss. "He also has burn marks on his neck and face, and all his fingers are crushed. Odd. I should have a better idea of what killed him when I complete my autopsy. All I can say now is that his death was, well, peculiar."

"Peculiar," Theiss echoed. "Dandy. You gonna write peculiar on the death certificate?" Theiss had known County Coroner Fred Pierce for the better part of ten years. He was a deliberate, methodical workman with a reputation for accuracy in determining the causes of death. Theiss quickly regretted his sarcasm.

The corpse was close to six feet tall and still well-built despite a slight paunch. Pierce and Theiss could not know that in life, Manigrove prided himself on his manly physique and a pencil thin mustache grown to offset the disturbing retreat of his hairline. But he was dead now, and nobody cared about his looks. He simply was a corpse with a secret.

"We better get some answers soon," the detective continued. "The army is giving me some heat and wants to be involved in this investigation. Beats the hell out of me why. This guy's army record is about as ordinary as they come. The only time he got hurt was in World War II, and that was when the recoil of cannon knocked him flat on his ass and broke a couple of his ribs. He got the Purple Heart for that. Can you believe it?" Theiss flipped through more of Manigrove's personnel file. "He sat out the Korean War at Fort Dix, New Jersey, first as a training company commander then as manager of the Officers Club.

"I noticed the rib damage was old stuff," Pierce replied, sticking to business. The coroner had served in the Army Medical Corps during World

War II, where he had treated enough injured men to know that it was futile to seek merit in suffering. All you could do was to heal and still the pain.

Theiss had been a ranger in World War II and won the Silver Star for extraordinary valor during the Battle of the Bulge. He was severely wounded and spent six months recuperating in an army hospital. He was recalled during Korea and was wounded again at Inchon. Men like Manigrove bugged him. But Manigrove was dead, and Theiss's job was to find out how, why and if it was murder.

As he left, the coroner turned his shaggy gray head toward the detective and, with a twinkle in his eye, asked: "Mike, is there a law against running over a dead man?" Theiss looked up and shrugged his shoulders.

2

THE CLAN

Albert Ruppert Manigrove III would have resented Theiss's harsh view of him. He had been a good soldier. He did everything asked of him. When he was told to be the liaison between his infantry company and an artillery battery during MacArthur's retaking of the Philippines, the young lieutenant did so with fear in his heart but a Manigrove determination to do his duty. If things had gone well, he would have been his company's next executive officer. But things did not go well. In the rush of battle, he had stepped too close to a cannon as it went off. It not only knocked him out and broke several ribs; it knocked him out of a battlefield promotion. Fate, as usual, seemed to work against him.

When the Korean Conflict broke out, he was assigned to train troops at Fort Dix, New Jersey. Promotion, he knew, rested in Korea, but safety rested at Fort Dix. He had seen enough of battle. When he was reassigned to run the base Officers

Club, he objected at first, feeling that the job was demeaning. This job did not seem to be an obvious route to promotion. But after a month there, he saw that the Officers Club did offer certain opportunities and, in the end, promotion.

The building was a ramshackle two-story affair, built in the 1930's as part of a Works Projects Administration exercise. The idea at the time was to teach jobless white-collar workers the building trades. The result was a barn-like structure that tilted slightly toward the west. Its floors creaked. Its plumbing leaked. And the lights occasionally went out. But all-in-all, it was a success. Its bar and kitchen functioned remarkably well.

It was a rowdy place, where officers of varying ranks mingled in liquored equality. The officer in charge of the club was to maintain a degree of order and ensure that no one became ill from the food or drink offered at too reasonable a price.

Manigrove found himself particularly suited for the job. Through tactical distributions of free booze, food, and coffee, he was able to minimize bar fights and the necessity to call in the Military Police. And he was innocuous. Nobody disliked Albert. Most didn't know his name.

Control of a building dedicated to privilege, relaxation and discreetness did open unexpected possibilities for Manigrove. The night of a holiday party, when a colonel asked if there was some room where he could take a young lady, Albert quickly obliged leading them to an upstairs storage room he had converted for his own romantic purposes. It contained a cot covered by a flower-print sheet and headed by a plump pillow of identical covering. A small lamp gave off a soft glow from its distant corner.

Manigrove added a bottle of scotch and two glasses for the colonel. An hour later, the colonel reappeared, smiling. "Albert, if there is anything I can do for you, my boy, just say so," he said.

"Could you get me promoted to captain?" Manigrove chanced.

The colonel's eyes twinkled. "I'll see what I can do," he replied.

A month later, Manigrove became a captain. After that, he augmented the storage room with a small bar that included a box of condoms.

There was another advantage to running the club, one that resonated with his Manigrove blood. He was in charge of buying the food, the liquor and anything else that had to be regularly replaced. The system of purchase was more relaxed than at the mess halls since much of the club's cost of operation was financed by dues the officers paid. Under the club's prior boss, vendors would bid to supply food and drink. The lowest price usually won the bid. Manigrove revised the system. The vendors would compete by offering him "an officer's incentive" as he put it. The one offering the largest incentive would win the bid. If the new process smacked of bribery or extortion, the vendors did not complain. They either reduced the quality of their products or raised their prices to offset their new costs. Manigrove opened a special bank account for himself and periodically sent a check to the "Manigrove Contributory Account," which gathered in funds from his family's various enterprises.

The Manigroves had been consumed with the making of money from the day they arrived in Charleston, South Carolina, as virtually impoverished French Huguenots. They made a lot of it since then. They profited as farmers, merchants, bankers, highwaymen and occasional pirates. They made fortunes in everything from bricks to indigo to cotton to dry goods to illegal alcohol.

An exception to their enterprise was the wholesale slave trade. They had declined to venture into that highly lucrative business because it ran against their convictions as victims of oppression themselves. Of course, while slavery did exist and was legal, they made the most of it using slave labor to turn profits in their various businesses.

"CARPE DIEM" was the family motto—"SEIZE THE DAY." Upon meeting each other, they might call out a paraphrase: "Exploit the opportunity," by way of greeting. Their industriousness made them part of the Lowcountry aristocracy—wealthy, respectable, conservative.

But Manigroves were marrying the Logares and the Laurens, the Moularies and the Gellards and other well-placed families. And they were begetting at geometric rates. By the mid-1800s, this expansion was creating a critical financial drag. The Manigrove wealth was dissipating through the sheer joy of procreation. The clan's traditional practice of giving newlyweds a portion of the family wealth was creating an ever-widening gap between income and spending. Funds for investment were being siphoned off to fulfill marriage vows. Something had to be done to stem the flow.

In what had been its custom since the dangerous days in France, the clan's elders met in periodic conclave to plan for the future. Since the development of Manigrove Plantation in the late 1700s, they held these conclaves in its spacious mansion. It stood near the Wando River, overlooking nearly 1,000 acres of the best indigo, rice, and brick producing land in the Lowcountry. More than 70 slaves toiled there, living in slave quarters, less than a quarter mile from the mansion and closer to the river. Docks jutted into the water from which boats carried Manigrove products to the Port of Charleston for shipment North or to Europe. Ancient, majestic oaks flourished around the structure as they did when the first Manigroves arrived to work the land in 1680. Multi-colored flowers spread for over an acre around the main house, carefully tended by slaves.

The mansion was all Old Charleston brick, topped by gothic-arched dominating chimneys. Its dining room held more than thirty people comfortably and its library fifty. The dining area was filled with mirrors to reflect as much light as possible on the long, dark serving table. Cabinets of deep walnut were filled with china and silverware from England and France.

The enormous library contained three large windows on each side, framed with pale blue satin curtains. An ivory-colored, gold-gilded grand piano, stood just below the staircase leading to the library.

It seemed small in the expanse of the reading room. At the far end, stood the fireplace, so wide and tall that several men could stand in it at one time. Its surrounding New England marble was carved with shepherds and their flocks, all bordered by an endless garland of perfect ivory-colored roses. In the warm days, petitioners to the clan's elders would huddle there, waiting their turn to be called. The petitioners often would gently rub the tiny marble figures in the hope that they would bring them luck on their requests. On chilly nights, the fireplace would be filled with blazing split logs, projecting a warm glow that not only comforted its recipients but cast long shadows up the rows of bookcases that extended to the tall ceiling.

Many of its books were histories of individual family members. Others wrote of the South and its constant striving for liberty, individual freedom and tradition. There was a portrait of Francis Marion, the Swamp Fox, who distinguished himself in the Revolution. There was a hand-written letter from Charles Pinckney, a signer of the Constitution, to Pierre Manigrove, founder of the American Manigrove line, thanking him for his financial and physical assistance in the War for Independence. Pierre nearly gave his life fighting with Marion at the battles of Nelson's Ferry, Black Mingo, and Tearcoat Swamp. He survived his wounds and lived to the ripe, old age of 90. In his memoirs, he wrote: "No matter how much blood we shed, the Manigroves can never repay our debt to this wondrous land that gave us freedom." Every subsequent Manigrove read that statement and held it as a fundamental belief.

On the night of December 28, 1850, the clan's elders met to resolve the issue of the family's growth and the possibility of war. "We have two issues before us," said bent, old Cyrus Manigrove, the most senior and shrewdest of the clan's hierarchy. "First, we must staunch the bleeding of our wealth. Second, we must deal with the dark clouds of conflict. My plan for the first is harsh in some respects and may limit our immediate objectives. But as always, we must survive before anything else." He paused for a moment, then continued. "If you are in agreement, we shall ban all marriages outside the Manigrove clan. Henceforth, Manigroves must marry their second and third cousins only. Those who refuse will be shunned and denied a share of the family's wealth. No one goes outside the family," he added for emphasis. "The family fortune stays locked within the family circle."

Only Jacob Manigrove, second to Cyrus in age and authority, offered objections. "I fear that it will cut us off from valuable connections with other influential families, and it will thicken the Manigrove blood. Too thick a soup becomes a tasteless porridge," he warned.

Cyrus eyed him with a cold eye. "We have made connections of marriage with all the best families, and we have ended up giving more than receiving. Our existing connections will remain for some time to come. Meanwhile, our treasury will gradually heal itself." He paused. "As to the thickening of our blood, I see only merit in that. Our offspring have shown themselves filled with talents. Intra-marriage can only enhance their skills." A murmur of approval filled the room. A show of hands confirmed Cyrus's proposal 11 to one. Only Jacob voted no. But he accepted the decision. Discipline, after all, gave the family its strength.

It had been a Manigrove rule since its flight from France that the proclamations of the clan's elders would be accepted by all members without question. Only this kind of single-minded unity could ensure the family would prevail first in safety and second in success. So, while some of the young, with eyes romantically set on outsiders, might grumble, they would obey. The clan's survival always came before the rights of an individual.

That settled, Cyrus moved on to a second concern. Calhoun had failed to block Congress's slave versus free state Compromise of 1850; he reminded the assemblage. "Mark me, this compromise has done nothing but place a thin bandage on a running sore. The South and the North will split over the slavery question, and war will happen. We all will fight to preserve the South. While we are not enamored of slavery, we are Southerners, and we are South Carolinians. We will do our duty." His voice was tired, heavy. He had weighed the possibilities of a war between the North and the South and could see nothing in the end but a total defeat of the South and a loss of profit for the family. The South's numbers were too small; its navy too weak and its manufacturing virtually nonexistent. The South's passion and skill at war could not make up for this.

And he did not share the belief that Northerners would cut and run when the first shots were fired.

In the end, the Manigroves must survive, he concluded, for in that survival rested the hopes of a re-born South.

"We must be prepared for the worst—that we will lose this war. Some things get destroyed in war. Later they get rebuilt. We must be prepared to be part of that reconstruction. We must create quiet alliances now with the businessmen and traders of the North. They will set the terms for the reconstruction of the new South, and we will be part of those terms."

This time, approval was unanimous. The family immediately began to reach toward the North. The importers and exporters of New York City were especially eager to work with the Manigroves, who offered concessions on their excellent products. The Manigroves, of course, did not limit themselves to New York City. They met with Northern politicians in Washington, allowing that these were but business discussions. Business bonds grew tight, friendships strong. Cyrus's foresight salvaged the family fortune after the Civil War. The Manigroves were called on to help the North rebuild the South, and many lucrative contracts went their way. Moreover, many Southerners later thanked the Manigroves for their capable handling of Reconstruction.

Inbreeding also worked well for a time. Several cousin marriages early on produced superior entrepreneurs. Another, oddly, produced a noted painter who, to the family's consternation, went to France to study with the great Impressionists. But inevitably genetic closeness took its toll. The Manigroves did not become physical bleeders, like European royalty. Instead, their wit and sharpness in matters of business gradually gave way to dullness. And they bled financially.

While they remained respected in the outside world for their still substantial wealth and historic power, the elders knew that a crisis was looming. The clan had survived the Great Depression. But fears of bankruptcy were rising.

Things were hardly better in 1935. Franklin Roosevelt, a Democrat, was in his third year in office. He had created an alphabet soup of agencies to help the poor. But he had done nothing to help the rich. The Republicans were empty of ideas and powerless. The Manigroves would have to rely upon the Manigroves. They knew unity and discipline gave them an inherent advantage over others. What was needed was fresh thinking. But inbreeding had robbed the elders of brilliant, dominant leaders. "We have become porridge as my grandfather warned," moaned Clyde Manigrove, grandson of Jacob Manigrove.

With no Cyrus to lead them, the patriarchs had substituted their theory of collective wisdom—the result of adding the intelligence of one elder to that of another. If one had an idea, he would not announce it. Instead, he would whisper it to his senior who would think about it and decide whether it was worthy of being passed on to yet a higher-ranked member. If the third in line believed it had merit, he would say it to a fourth. When this process reached the fifth in line, it became his decision as to whether the idea merited an open debate. If so, he would announce: "I have accepted an idea for debate." Often, the version of the idea ultimately debated was a considerable departure from that offered by its initiator, but that was its beauty. It was the resultant of collective wisdom.

Strengthened by the knowledge that collective wisdom would resolve their problems, they returned to the family mansion in early December 1935. After a sumptuous dinner, surrounded by generations of Manigroves, the elders retired to the vast library for deliberations. One decision was that cousin marriage would be abolished. It had worked well for a time, but it had become a drag on the collective future. "Our youth are no longer vigorous. I can find no genius among them, not even an innovative scoundrel. They lack the brains and audacity that made this family great," said Rufus Manigrove speaking for the three-fourths majority needed to rescind a family rule. "Marriage outside the family will refresh its juices, thin its too-thick blood," he continued. "Besides, the outsiders have more, and we have less. We will receive more than we will give. We have nothing to lose."

3

DUTY CALLS

Young Albert Ruppert Manigrove III heard all this from the hallway where he had hidden within a huge grandfather clock. From there, he heard the vote that abolished cousin marriage. Though his father and mother were second cousins, he did not believe it had hampered him. "Five fingers and toes," he told himself. "College graduate. Not bad looking, healthy. And we're as smart as the old guys." Besides, at 21, he was not considering marriage in or outside the Manigrove clan. "Play the field, be a lady's man," he thought to himself. "Now, that's a career!"

He had been steeling himself for the next portion of the annual conclave. It had long been a tradition that when a Manigrove reached 21, the elders would decide that individual's business career. And, according to the accompanying ritual, those about to be inducted into the family's business enterprises would serve as attendants at the grand meeting. This would ensure that no indiscreet helper would hear the deliberations. As was appropriate for such solemn events, the attendants dressed mostly in dark colors. Men in a dark suit, quiet tie, white shirt, dark shoes that laced and dark socks. Women wore dark business suits with dark hats, white gloves and low heels on dark shoes. Once they attended the elders, they would leave for distant parts of the mansion to await summoning.

This night Albert dutifully served the drinks and light sweets indulged in by the elders at these meetings. His eyes were appropriately down, not daring to look even at his beloved grandfather, Albert Ruppert Manigrove, Sr. After serving, he quickly and silently departed. But instead of going to some distant part of the house, he moved to the side of the great grandfather clock that stood against the hallway wall adjoining the library.

It was an ancient timepiece whose workings were created by a master clockmaker. Its housing was exquisitely carved by a Renaissance artist in the Rococo style. Albert hesitated for just a moment then pulled the head of a jutting gargoyle. Instantly, a panel slid silently away, revealing a secret closet. He had discovered it years ago as a child when he bumped his head against the tiny sculpture jutting from the clock's ornate enclosure. He had yanked at it for revenge. And it revealed its hideaway. He had supposed it was built there to store treasure or perhaps hurriedly needed rifles. But it was empty when he found it. Now, he could just squeeze into it and listen. He was surprised how clear the voices in the library were. Then he spotted the little spy hole that ran through the wall into the library. Near the hole, he noticed two crudely carved letters—not simply letters but the initials C.M.

"Cyrus Manigrove," Albert whispered to himself. "That old dog. He set up a way so he could spy on the other elders. Or maybe, it was before he was an elder himself, and he just wanted to hear what was going on, like me. Bet I take after that old dog," he went on, with a silent chuckle. As the clock ticked loudly above him, he waited for what would come next.

The conclave's collective wisdom decided that the latest line of maturing Manigroves should be diversified, like a good stock portfolio. All would have to be placed in jobs that would lead to solid returns for the family. Winston had shown a feeling for the retail business. Dry goods would be a good place for him. One of the DuSheys ran a string of boutiques across the South. Manigroves had married DuSheys often before the cousin rule. There still were good blood ties. "I know Maurice DuShey very well," said Rufus. "I'm sure I can get him to place Winston in one of his stores. That boy already has shown a talent for women's clothes. Mostly taking them off," he said laughing. The other old men cackled in response.

Paul, who was always borrowing money from someone, would become a banker. Franklin, who liked to play in dirt and grow sunflowers, would be a farmer and Octavia, a real estate agent. The family owned land throughout South Carolina. She could be an asset in the buying and selling of properties. She was not overly bright, but she had shown herself to be a dogged worker throughout her school career. She was attractive as well. And looks could help in the business world. "Good legs have proven better than the best sales pitch in convincing a buyer," mumbled ancient Byron Manigrove. Real estate also would give her time to get married and raise a family.

Finally, the discussion came to Albert.

Surely, Grandpa Albert would come up with something good, perhaps banking or managing one of the family's small hotels, young Albert thought. Grandpa Albert was now a middle elder, with some influence.

He saw Grandpa Albert pull hard on his cigar. "I've talked to my son about this a bit," he said, "and we've come to the conclusion that Albert would make a fine soldier."

"A soldier?" Albert gasped.

"A soldier?" Mendel Manigrove snorted. "Now what use do we have for a soldier? Where's the profit in that?" he asked.

"Now, there are ways and ways of making a profit," Grandpa Albert responded. "Young Albert hasn't shown himself to have any par-ticular interests or hobbies, but he did make it through the Citadel, a rigorous military college as you know. Not the best grades, but he made the drill team, and he looks sharp in a uniform. The way my son and I look at it, young Albert could spend a few years in the service and then begin a career in politics. A man who looks good in a uniform makes a terrific candidate for office, and the Mani-groves have not had an elected official in 30 years or more." He waited for his argument to sink in and then added the hammer. "You know that elected officials dole out contracts and commissions and important jobs, and all of these would come the Manigrove way."

It made sense. With Roosevelt pump-priming the nation, contracts and big loans to businesses were going this way and that. A couple of years in the service to get some pictures in uniform, and Albert would be a perfect candidate for office.

"Who cares about soldiers?" Mendel Manigrove shot back. "We are at peace. The army is tiny. Who is going to vote for someone because he wore a uniform?

"True," Grandpa Albert responded, "but there is trouble brewing in Europe. That man Hitler is building guns and tanks. Mark me, he will force the hands of the Brits and Frenchies, and we will be drawn into it. And that means a bigger army."

Rumors of war in Europe had been growing. The elders sipped their brandy, puffed their cigars and pondered. "Having a soldier might be a good investment," Josiah Manigrove finally said. He was the most senior of the elders and had their respect. "Even if he never runs for public office."

Collective wisdom concluded that Albert should become an officer and a gentleman and move on to elective office as soon as possible. It was not a choice young Albert wanted to hear, but he knew there was little he could do about it. As was the custom, he and the others were brought in one by one to hear their fates and offer objections, if any. But never had objections from juniors led the elders to overturn a decision. The young would contribute as they were told and in return receive a proportionate share of the clan's wealth.

Young Albert had barely made it out of his hiding place in the clock when his name was called by helpers stationed on each floor of the mansion. He made no objection to the military-political career staked out for him, though he advised the elders that he was not much for heroics.

"America isn't at war, and it is not going to war," Grandpa Albert responded, his eyes twinkling with satisfaction at a well-made decision. "No need for heroics. Your name, the Manigrove name, will be on billboards one day from here to the Georgia line," he added.

"Yes sir," answered Albert respectfully. He liked the idea of his name on billboards. But a voice inside his head kept saying he would rather have been in retail, like Cousin Winston or banking like Cousin Paul.

4

KLUGMAN'S CASE

Joey Klugman had been sitting in Colonel Hoffner's waiting room for perhaps ten minutes before Hoffner's aide, First Sergeant Terrance McDonald, said, "He wants you." The ten minutes had not been entirely wasted. Klugman had flipped through several fly-fishing magazines, from which he learned that the colonel was an avid fly fisherman. He also had scanned the top of McDonald's desk for bits and pieces when the first sergeant briefly left the room. Klugman was good at reading upside down and backward. He had learned these skills putting out a weekly newspaper in his college years. His brief scan of McDonald's desk identified Hoffner's current visitors as FBI Special Agents Laurens and Conrad.

"The CID is moving in fancy circles," he thought to himself. The Criminal Investigation Division, to which Klugman belonged, most closely resembled a police department's detective division, except its jurisdiction wasn't a city or a town or a county. It was the entire United States Army and any outside territory the army might occupy. It worked everything from thefts to homicides to bank robberies, burglaries, drug buys, and domestic violence.

But unlike ordinary police departments, it also investigated cases of suspected treason. With a raging Cold War and a military rife with secret ordnance and technology, more and more of the CID's time was being taken up with checking on espionage and betrayal. In 1950, Senator Joseph McCarthy of Wisconsin had claimed there were Communists in the State Department. Earlier, Klaus Fuchs, a physicist who had worked on the atom bomb, turned out to be a Soviet spy. By the mid-1950s, the Cold War had shifted from peripheral military engagements like Korea to a head-to-head technological struggle where the scientists were the warriors and secrecy an obsession.

The CID was well equipped for its broad range of investigations. It had forensic scientists and highly sophisticated equipment as well as fingerprint, crime and convict files. It also could turn to the Federal Bureau of Investigation and other federal agencies if help were needed. Its elite cadre was being trained at its school at Fort Belvoir.

The giant swordfish tacked to the colonel's back wall didn't surprise Klugman. Neither did Special Agent Mark Laurens—a tall, crew-cut Southerner whose muscular frame seemed crammed into his suit. He expected someone like that, cut from J. Edgar Hoover's all-American mold. Special Agent Anita Conrad, however, was another matter. She was not so much pretty as sensual, a package that when taken together made a man wonder how wild she would be in bed. She clearly was not out of the Hoover cookie cutter. Both stood up as Klugman entered the room. "Master Sergeant Klugman," the colonel announced. He threw Hoffner a sharp salute. He then grasped Laurens' and Conrad's hands firmly. He thought Conrad's was especially warm. "Please call me Joey," he said, mostly to her.

Klugman had met Hoffner just once before and very briefly at his graduation from CID's investigative program. Hoffner, he recalled, gave the commencement speech. It had to do with the special responsibility the graduates had to the army and the country. They were to remember that no matter how mighty the United States military was, its members were not above the law. "We will ensure that the army sets an example as a democratic institution," he said. He also reminded the new detectives that they must show no fear or favor to high-ranking authorities. "Rank has no status in an investigation," he said. "You report and are responsible only to your CID commander, and he is responsible only to the provost marshal general. And the provost marshal general," he continued, "reports only to people pretty close to God." Klugman had liked that. At least he was in a stateside unit that didn't have to take any crap.

Klugman's class was unusual for the army, a result of the grinding end of the Korean War. The draft was continuing, but there was little need for more infantry, armored or artillery battalions. The Army Chief of Staff decided that highly educated draftees and enlistees with special backgrounds would be assigned to elite units such as the CID. In addition, CID detectives would be career soldiers. All 30 members of Klugman's graduating class were college graduates who had distinguished them-selves in World War II and Korean battlefields and had decided to remain in the service. They loved their country, respected the army and craved the excitement that only the military offered.

Unlike the FBI, the CID did not have its origins as a force to combat organized crime nationwide. Its roots grew from the soil of the Civil War draft riots, which occurred mainly in New York City. At the height of that war, in 1863, Congress passed the "Enrollment Act," the nation's first draft law. The law, however, had one large loophole. A man could avoid compulsory military service by paying the government $300 to hire a substitute. Thus, the draft's greatest impact was on the poor, many of whom were immigrants living in New York City. They had little relish for a war they barely under-stood and a foe they hardly knew. To many of them, the draft made the struggle "a rich man's war and a poor man's fight." Added to this was New York City's general animosity toward a war that closed trade with Southern merchants, such as the Man-igroves, who had filled its wharfs with goods for manufacture and transport to other parts of the world. The poor men rioted. The business commu-nity turned its back. And the Union Army had to be called in to restore order.

Shaken by the riots, Secretary of War Edwin Stanton created the Provost Marshal General's Bureau. Its duty was to enforce the draft law. That bureau eventually mothered the Army's Military Police Corps from which the Criminal Investigation Division was born. All of which, Klugman learned during his induction into this unique body.

"Sergeant, I have called you in to investigate a rather unusual death," the colonel said. "A Captain Albert Ruppert Manigrove III was found dead on the Dixie Highway about halfway between his base at Fort Knox, Kentucky and the city of Louisville. He clearly had been struck by a large vehicle, but, according to the county coroner those injuries were not the cause of his death. He died because his nervous system was pulled apart."

"A disease?" Joey ventured.

"None that we are aware of," Hoffner replied. "Ordinarily, we would pursue this with our people at Fort Knox and the local police. But because of, shall I say, the sensitive unit to which Capitan Manigrove belonged, the provost marshal decided to bring in an off-campus investigator, so to speak."

"And I'm it."

"You are it," the colonel responded with emphasis.

Joey looked up at the large silvery fish tacked to Hoffner's wall, and suddenly felt great sympathy for it. "If this thing goes sour," he thought, "I'm the fish." Aloud he asked: "What's so sensitive about this unit?"

"Excuse me, Colonel," Agent Laurens interrupted. "Does the sergeant have Q clearance?"

Hoffner stared at the six-foot-one-inch Laurens with one of those hard-eyed, hard-assed looks that cut down subordinates. He was nearly as tall as Laurens and, except for age, was nearly as chiseled. He clearly was not intimidated by the FBI man. "Do you think that I would have brought in an agent who didn't have the highest clearance?"

"Well, no sir," came the reply. "But I felt I had a duty to ask."

"Consider that you have done your duty," Hoffner shot back.

Two thoughts raced through Joey's mind. First that Anita Conrad cracked the slightest of smiles at Laurens' dressing down. Second, that just maybe Hoffner was Jewish. The hard ass part tilted toward German ancestry. The answering a question with a question tilted toward Jewish. It was a way of thinking that went back a thousand years to the ancient rabbis. Either way, he liked the colonel. He could share a fighting hole with this man.

Hoffner already had moved on. "Manigrove's was a non-science officer attached to the 8-8-5-2 Technical Service Unit. It, in turn, is—on paper—part of the Medical Service Corps. The 8-8-5-2, however, offers no services to the fort's hospital even though it is located nearby. Its personnel has no contact with the tank division based at Fort Knox or with the basic training regiments located there. And it has nothing to do with the gold stored there. It is one unit of something called the Army Medical Research Laboratory. Its assignments come directly from the Pentagon, and its findings go directly to the Pentagon. It is linked to similar units throughout the country.

"Because of the secret nature of its work, the 8-8-5-2 is surrounded by razor wire fences that separate it from the rest of Fort Knox. There is only one way into it and one way out. It is guarded by members of a ranger battalion. No one enters or leaves without showing special identification, including the fort's commanding general. The guards answer only to the head of the unit, Lieutenant Colonel Francis X. Doyle, and the base commandant, Major General Horatio Stockton."

"And what was Manigrove's role in all this?" Joey asked.

"He was in charge of all enlisted personnel activities outside of their scientific work," the colonel responded.

"In other words, the barracks, the latrines, the mess hall, the uniforms," Joey said.

"Right."

"So, he had nothing to do with the secret stuff?" Klugman continued.

"We have been told no," answered Hoffner. "But he did have access to the entire facility and had secret clearance. That's what scares us. The Soviets would be very interested in what goes on at the 8-8-5-2. And that's where our friends at the FBI come in."

The colonel motioned toward Laurens, giving him permission to talk. "We have received reports that someone has been supplying information from this facility to the Soviets," Laurens said. "The information being supplied is good and very current. It also covers several subjects being researched at this unit, indicating that the supplier has access to every part of the facility."

"We also believe that the Soviets were most interested in the work being done on radiation," added Conrad.

"Radiation?" Joey said in surprise. "I thought that stuff was being handled by the atom bomb folks at Los Alamos."

"Much of it is," Conrad broke in. "But there is so much we don't know that other scientific units within the government have been called in to assist. The 8-8-5-2 is one of the facilities the government has working on the problem."

"And that's where you come in," Joey said, turning toward the agent.

"Right. I am a doctor reassigned from the Atomic Energy Commission to the FBI to work on atomic espionage."

"I see," said Joey. He then turned back to Hoffner. "I just want to be clear, sir, am I running this investigation or is the FBI?"

"You are running it under my supervision. You report directly to me. Laurens and Conrad are here to give you technical support and more juice if the local brass gets in the way. Civilians aren't in the chain of command. But I expect you to keep them apprised of developments and to employ them in whatever way will help. I'm not looking for the Lone Ranger, Klugman."

"Clear, sir," Joey replied. He had an idea how Conrad could help, but he could live without the muscular Laurens, he thought.

Hoffner looked at the two FBI agents. "Just so you understand, Sergeant Klugman is one of my most qualified investigators. He has solved a couple of major cases for us, and he's gotten in harm's way to do so. He is a college graduate who was at the top of his class at CID school. He wears a Silver

Star, a Purple Heart, and a Combat Infantryman's Badge. Most important, and the main reason I assigned him this case, is he thinks outside the box." The colonel paused while Joey looked down at his shoes. He liked the resume, but he felt Hoffner was trying too hard to sell him to his new associates.

Laurens and Conrad stared at Klugman without revealing their thoughts.

5

THE GENERAL

The Dixie Highway that leads to Fort Knox is one of those roads whose romantic name conceals a murderous reality. Its treacherous ways have proven to be deadly, seductive traps for hard driving, hard drinking soldiers eager to leave Fort Knox or return to it before their passes ran out. Locals called it "The Dixie Dieway."

It also was the road on which the body of Captain Albert Ruppert Manigrove III had been found. But as the investigative team drove the highway shortly before noon, it seemed just another busy thoroughfare.

As Mark Laurens finally eased his unmarked FBI sedan up to the Fort Knox guard gate, an MP moved out smartly and asked his destination at the Fort.

"The commanding general's office," Laurens replied. "We have an appointment with the general."

The MP re-entered the guard box, checked a sheet and asked for individual identifications. Having verified that they were expected and that they appeared to be who they said they were, he gave them directions and raised the blocking bar. As they had throughout the trip, they rotated seat assignments, so the driver always had company in the front passenger seat. As they entered the fort, the MP passed a quizzical look at the sergeant sitting in the back being driven by two important civilian visitors.

It had taken them most of the morning to drive down from Fort Belvoir, Md., to the outskirts of Fort Knox, where they checked into a small motel. They had adjoining rooms with Anita Conrad's in the middle. Immediately after checking in, they headed for Fort Knox to make their 1300 hours appointment with its commanding officer, Major General Horatio Stockton. This was to be a courtesy call, nothing more.

As they entered his office, Horatio Stockton rose. He was a short, bulky man dressed in pressed green fatigues and wearing a pearl-handled .38 caliber revolver. Joey saluted and came to attention. The general saluted back and said, "At ease, Sergeant." He then turned and shook the hands of the two civilians.

Joey remembered "Shorty" Stockton as a brave, sometimes reckless, leader of the Third Infantry Division. During his stint in Korea, he was known as much for his pistol and wild jeep rides as he was for his tactics.

Stockton turned back to Joey. "I recognize you. I remember pinning that Silver Star on your chest," he said. "Brave man," he added, turning to the FBI agents. "He saved a lot of soldiers' lives. I don't know why a good combat soldier would want to become a cop. But that's his affair. Now, let's get down to business. You are here to find out whether there is any connection between Captain Manigrove's death and what goes on at that secret, little rat's nest he helped supervise."

"Yes sir," Joey responded.

"I'll give you as much support as you need," the general went on. "But my authority ends where the nest's barbed wire begins. Once inside there, you are on your own."

"We'd like to begin by examining the personnel files of every member of that unit," Joey replied.

"My exec, Colonel Freeman, will see to that," Stockton said.

"What can you tell us informally about Lieutenant Colonel Francis X. Doyle?"

"Doyle is in command of the 8-8-5-2's scientific work. He is brilliant, mad as a hatter and as irreverent to military protocol, practice, and discipline as the rest of his motley crew. I know only that they do secret experimentation and that Doyle has made it a point of denying me any information on what the hell is going on there. On top of that, he turns a blind eye to the flagrant disregard of his men for military order and discipline. I sent Manigrove in there to shape up the enlisted men who, at least, must live by army rules once outside that barbed wire."

"Why did you pick Manigrove?" Laurens asked.

Stockton paused before replying. "I try to be a good judge of men. If you are to survive in combat, you must have a sense of who is going to stick with you and who is going to bug out. You also must have an eye for each man's talents and weaknesses.

Manigrove was a misfit as a career officer. He fought well when he had to fight, but he didn't enjoy it. It may be an ugly reality, hard for a civilian to understand, but a real officer loves war. That aside, Manigrove was a lost soul. In an army, you are surrounded by people you like and don't like. As a commanding officer, you must relate to them and utilize them to the army's best advantage. Emotion can't get in the way. Manigrove spent 19 years in the military. Nobody liked him or hated him, including me. In the case of the enlisted men at the 8-8-5-2, I thought that might be an advantage. They have proved to be an exception to the like/don't like rule. Those men have seduced the officers who liked them and foiled the officers who disliked them. They are not ordinary. They were sent to this special unit because they held one or more graduate degrees, mostly in the hard sciences. Some are officers. Most are draftees who see the Army as one big dictatorship that has interfered with their lives."

"You are saying you picked Manigrove because he was neutral?" Laurens persisted.

The general paused, unaccustomed to being questioned. "It was also because I had nobody else. Korea was chewing up the officer corps. I was at the bottom of the barrel. And the man Manigrove replaced over there was retiring. It didn't cost me anything to throw him in with that gang of smart-assed misfits. So, two good reasons. Simple as that."

"Sounds to me like you were throwing him to the wolves," the FBI man responded.

"There are always going to be wolves," the general snapped back.

"Thank you for your time, sir," Joey cut in. "Agents Laurens and Conrad will go through the personnel files."

The three rose to leave. But the general was not quite through. "One more thing, Sergeant," he said. "I expect to be fully briefed by you on the progress of this investigation."

"I will keep you apprised, sir, within the limits of the discretion given me by my superiors," Joey answered.

"I am your superior," the general replied.

"You're not in my chain of command, sir," Joey replied. He saluted, about faced and followed the FBI agents out the door.

6

MEETING DOYLE

Joey Klugman decided to walk from the commanding general's headquarters to the 8-8-5-2. The half mile would give him time to think. And there were beginning to be lots of questions. Did General Stockton have more than a turf interest in this case? Did he really pick Manigrove because he was the bottom of the barrel? And, of course, that big, nagging question: What could have torn Manigrove's insides apart?

"Hi-Di, Hi-Di, Hi-Di-Ho.
Only two more years to go."
"SOUND OFF!"
"One, Two."
"SOUND OFF!"
"Three, Four."
"BREAK IT ON DOWN"
"One, Two, Three, Four,
One, Two
"THREE-FOUR."

Joey looked up. The surprise wasn't the platoon of recruits marching toward him.

It was the voice and then the sight of their sergeant.

"Tony Villano!" Joey shouted. Tony was as small, trim, and agile as when he last saw him as they fought for their lives on the banks of the Han River in Korea.

Tony broke into a huge smile and halted his platoon. "C'mon over!" he called.

Then, turning to the recruits, he said, "This is a real soldier, a real sonofabitch of a soldier. He saved my friggin' life. Say 'Hello, Master Sergeant Klugman', real loud."

"Hello, Sergeant Klugman," some 60 voices sung out.

"LOUDER!" screamed Tony Villano.
"HELLO MASTER SERGEANT KLUGMAN! "
"LOUDER!"
"HELLO, MASTER SERGEANT KLUGMAN!"

"Now that's better," Villano said, a broad smile lighting his face.

"I couldn't see you 'til I looked down," Klugman chirped.

"Jew bastard, wise ass," the five-foot-six-inch Tony shot back. "Good thing the Skinny Guinea loves you. Otherwise, you swim with the fish." Then he rushed Joey, grabbed him in a bear hug and yelled, "Damn, it's good to see you!" Joey was three inches taller and 30 pounds heavier. But Tony yanked him off his feet with ease.

"Now that they put you back together, you're as strong as ever," Klugman managed.

"Stronger. I work out every day so that I can beat the crap out of these recruits," Villano answered, dropping his friend to the ground. Then he studied Joey. "Class A uniform, a bunch of rockers to go with your sergeant stripes. And a brass insignia I don't recognize. What's up? What you doing in this hell hole?"

Joey thought for a second. "Now don't take this the wrong way, but I'm a cop—a detective in the Army Criminal Investigation Division." He took a step back as he talked half expecting Tony to throw a punch. After all, Tony had bragged about his mob connections in Korea. "You want some fighting?" he would say. "Come down to President Street in Brooklyn. We'll show you some real fighting."

"A cop? No, shit. Hey, that's okay. In Brooklyn, we know how to deal with cops. We cut them in for a piece of the action."

Joey felt relieved. "I'm here because some Captain got killed out on the Dixie Highway and the local police need a hand. That's it. End of story. I'll be around for a couple of weeks. Let's throw down a couple of beers and talk about old times. Hey, you know anything about this guy? His name was Manigrove."

"Just what I read in the papers, I don't know much else. This is a big place," Tony responded. "But let's get those beers." They exchanged phone numbers. Joey thought Tony's eyes flickered just a bit at his mention of Manigrove's name.

"All right, you recruits, say goodbye to Master Sergeant Klugman, nice and loud," Villano ordered.

"GOODBYE, MASTER SERGEANT KLUGMAN," 60 voices screamed.

Joey waved at the platoon and walked on. The road was wide and dusty, and far away he could hear the familiar rumble of tanks. Then off to his right, he spotted the 8-8-5-2.

A high fence topped with razor wire surrounded the enclave of eight two-story buildings. Shrubs blocked most of the view. But he could see a large, black steel drum that stood perhaps 20 feet high and 15 feet wide. Painted along its sides were sets of three bright yellow triangles rounded at their corners. He also caught parts of a large red word painted on the drum: "DANGER," it said.

He slowed his pace to get a better look at the unit's interior. He caught glimpses of young men moving about in a variety of un-military dress. Some wore conventional Class A uniforms; only their shoes were penny loafers. Others wore fatigues and red-topped sneakers. Still, others were in white or green hospital scrubs, but again the footwear was casual, in many cases flip flops. Socks ranged from government issue to striking argyles. Hats too ranged from army caps to cowboy to none. It was clear why General Stockton was furious at their less than military appearance. They were defying him under the protection he had been forced to supply the 8-8-5-2. "It must be driving Stockton nuts," Joey thought with a chuckle.

He was up to the turn in the road that led to the guard booth. As he approached, a soldier stepped out carrying an M2 Carbine. He was big all around, from height to shoulders to bulky thighs and large booted feet. He was all mean business.

"Your pass," he said in a crisp, accented voice.

Klugman pulled out the special, laminated pass that Colonel Hoffner had given him and the FBI agents. "Freshly minted for you at the Pentagon. Guaranteed to get you in anywhere," he had said. But the colonel evidently had not talked to the guard at the 8- 8-5-2.

"Not valid," the guard said.

"Not valid?" Joey asked in surprise.

"It doesn't have Colonel Doyle's stamp," the guard replied.

"It doesn't require the lieutenant colonel's stamp," Joey responded. He enjoyed emphasizing Doyle's light colonel status. A full colonel is on track for general. A light colonel, who remains a light colonel for any length of time, is on track for retirement. "This was issued by the Department of Defense and signed by the Deputy Secretary of Defense, who is the only individual authorized to sign such high-security passes."

The bulky guard seemed to swell up even larger. "No stamp, no entry," he said jutting out an already belligerent jaw. His accent had become more pronounced. Joey instinctively glanced at the guard's nametag. "Franz Ludaniczech,"it said.

Joey stepped back a foot to be out of the way of a butt stroke should the guard decide such a measure was necessary. Klugman smiled. "We can do this two ways," he said. "You can call Lieutenant Colonel Doyle and tell him the situation. Or, I can call my full bird colonel at the Criminal Investigation Division, who will call the Secretary of Defense's office, and in no time, you will be shoveling whales' turds on some Aleutian Island beach. And I will be inside Lt. Colonel Doyle's office backed by one of this Fort's tanks."

The guard's eyes widened just a bit. He was a brute, but he was dumb. He needed just one more push.

"Look, ordinarily, I'm a nice guy and let a lot of things slide. But you are in violation of the Army's Code of Military Justice, Article 21-18, which says it is a crime to hamper a criminal investigation, which you are doing. I should point out that this is a felony punishable by up to five years in a federal prison and loss of all benefits—and any chance of citizenship. Your lieutenant colonel is in violation of a separate article involving the creation of bogus military documents. Now, which way is it going to be? Do I get in, or do you go to jail?" he asked, flashing his CID badge for emphasis.

The guard wavered, then wilted. He reached for the booth's phone. "This is Corporal Ludaniczech at the gate. There is a Master Sergeant Joseph Klugman here from the CID demanding entrance. He has a pass, but it doesn't have the colonel's stamp. What shall I do?" There was a long pause. Then the guard turned back to Joey. "The colonel's aide says you can't come in without the stamp."

"Tell him if he doesn't change his mind, he will be facing at least five years in jail, and when that tank arrives, I will personally handcuff him to it," Joey answered.

The guard transmitted the message. Again, there was a pause. Finally, "She says you can enter, but you will have to be escorted to Colonel Doyle's office."

"She?" asked Joey.

"She, as in second lieutenant hot bitch," the guard answered with a smirk. "You'll see."

Minutes later, two GI's arrived by jeep. They carried carbines as well as side arms. They got out and motioned Joey to walk between them. They walked briskly down the block toward Doyle's office. As they neared the squat brown building, the guard on Joey's left half whispered, "Korea, huh?" He had glimpsed the decorations on Joey's uniform.

"'Yeah," Klugman replied. "Third Infantry Division-Han River."

"Fifty-sixth RCT, Pusan breakout," the guard answered. Then he glanced at the lieutenant colonel's office, where a red light blinked outside. "Red means he's pissed off. Nobody usually goes in when red is on. Be careful. He's nuts."

"Thanks," Joey said, as he entered. He noted that the guards took up posts on each side of the front door.

Inside, he first saw a guard's "hot bitch." She was the Women's Army Corps Lieutenant, who served as the colonel's aide. She had raven hair and deep blue-green eyes that seemed to shimmer. Her figure was not so much proportioned as sculpted. As she looked at Klugman, he felt a shiver of sexual desire. "Gorgeous," he thought.

"Please take a seat, Master Sergeant," she said.

Joey managed, "Thank you, Lieutenant." Then he added, "Can I call you something besides Lieutenant?"

"Sir would work just fine," she replied in what Joey recognized as a New York or at worst New Jersey accent.

"You from New York?" he tried.

Just then the red light directly above Doyle's office stopped blinking, and a steady green light came on. "What is this guy's fascination with traffic lights," Joey wondered.

Gorgeous smiled her sensual smile and said: "The colonel will see you now, Sergeant."

Doyle's office surprised Joey. While most ranking officers allowed themselves the luxury of personalizing their inner sanctums, Doyle's was empty of anything personal. No pictures of family, no books, other than technical references, no memorabilia, no flags, nothing to reveal the inner man. Joey had always looked for such clues to the minds of those he was investigating. "He is concealing himself," Joey thought.

The lieutenant colonel did not look up as Joey entered. Klugman snapped to attention and threw him a salute. Doyle continued to ignore him, looking down at some papers on his desk. After a minute had passed, Joey decided Doyle was playing a head game, making him feel uncomfortable, showing him who was really in charge. He decided to end it. "Master Sergeant Joseph Klugman, Criminal Investigation Division, assigned to the Deputy Secretary of Defense," he said, in a loud voice.

It got Doyle's attention. He rose or seemed to float out of his seat like some tall, wispy ghost. He was a good six feet six inches tall and rail thin, weighing perhaps 170 pounds. His face was pale as if it rarely saw sunlight, and his cheekbones jutted from narrow cavities below impenetrable gray eyes. "I don't give a damn who you're assigned to.

You don't come in here and bullshit my people and try to bullshit me," he said.

Joey was impressed. The man was tough and smart. But so was Joey. "Violating army regulations is not bullshit, even if you are a high-ranking officer, sir," he responded. "You may have rank, Lieutenant Colonel, but I have the authority to arrest anyone, regardless of rank, who is in violation of military law."

"Are you threatening me?" asked Doyle.

"I am just stating the facts, sir."

"We will see who arrests whom around here. I am charging you with insubordination and disrespect for command." With that, Doyle pressed the button on his intercom and said, "Have the guards come in and arrest the master sergeant."

Lieutenant Gorgeous hesitated, then replied: "Sir, the gate just called to say two FBI agents are demanding to enter. They said they are working with Sergeant Klugman. They have non-stamped passes, just like the master sergeant. What shall I tell the guard?"

Doyle looked as if he'd touched an electric wire. "The FBI? Why wasn't I told?" he asked no one in particular. "Forget the guards. Tell the gate to delay the FBI agents for a minute and then direct them to my office. No escorts. I'm not hard to find." Then, he looked at Klugman with renewed interest. "Just what the hell do you and the FBI want? Everything here is secret. We can't have outside people stumbling around here. And this is not about stamps on passes."

"No, sir," Joey replied. "This is about the strange death of Captain Albert Ruppert Manigrove III."

7

MANGROVE'S PROBLEM

Doyle slumped back in his chair, looking wary. He had thought this visit had somehow been arranged by General Stockton as part of his constant campaign to get rid of him. Stockton earlier had triggered visits from the Army's Inspector General's Office and the Surgeon General's Office. The inspectors had found the 8-8-5-2's scientific work all in order. He had expected harassment, but this was of a different order, bigger. The Defense Department, the CID, and the FBI were involved this time. Stockton could reach out to the Pentagon. But his reach was not that long and not that powerful. This was not Stockton. He would have to be careful. He would have to change tactics, be more cooperative, less aggressive. But this pushy sergeant annoyed him. An enlisted man with power. Dangerous.

The lieutenant colonel pressed his intercom and again ordered, "Have the FBI people directed to my office. No escorts. And tell those two in front of my building that they are dismissed."

Then his deep-set eyes looked squarely at Joey. "Perhaps we should wait until your superiors arrive," he said.

"They report to me," Joey shot back. "But you may as well save your breath until they arrive."

Doyle snorted and looked down at the papers on his desk. Moments later, Laurens and Conrad arrived. They were surprised to see Joey standing since there were three chairs in the room facing the lieutenant colonel's desk. But they had no time to think about it. A congenial, courtly Doyle reached out for their hands. "Please, be seated," he said. "All of you."

Joey was happy to drop into a chair. His feet were hurting. But he was also quick to retake the initiative. "As I said, Lieutenant Colonel, we are looking into the death of Captain Manigrove. The county coroner is unhappy with his findings. It seems the captain was torn apart internally. He does not know whether this was the result of an accident or occurred by design. But someone tried to cover up the death by running his body over with a truck." Joey paused, letting his information sink in. Then he continued, "Since the captain was assigned to this very sensitive outfit, the CID and the FBI have been ordered to determine the cause of death and whether it had anything to do with his role here. I know you will give us your full cooperation, sir."

"Yes, of course," Doyle responded, his face a mask.

"You can start by giving us complete access to your facility. If that means putting your personal stamp on our passes, please do so. As you can see from our passes, we are cleared for secret information."

"I will tell my aide to stamp your passes when you leave," the lieutenant colonel said.

"Next, we want you to order your staff, both technical and administrative, to answer all of our questions. Special Agent Conrad is an expert in a variety of scientific disciplines. Agent Laurens holds degrees in mechanical engineering and law."

"And you, Sergeant?" asked Doyle. "What qualifies you to ask questions and understand answers?"

"My authority from the Deputy Secretary of Defense qualifies me to ask questions, and my two colleagues will make sure I understand all the answers," Joey replied. Laurens and Conrad shifted uneasily in their seats.

"Come, come. You are modest," Doyle said. "I checked you out while you were baiting the guard at the gate. I know you hold degrees in Psychology and English. And you were at the top of your class at CID school. Pity, you didn't become an officer."

"I wouldn't have made much of a gentleman," Joey said. Doyle looked at him with something that could be hate or—amusement—in his eyes.

Laurens mercifully broke in. "What can you tell us about Captain Manigrove, officially and off the record?" he asked

"On or off the record, I can tell you, you should be asking General Stockton about Manigrove. He was the general's man, not mine. The general removed his predecessor and assigned him to me. He directed that Manigrove be given full access to the facility. But I'll say this: The captain did try to do his job making the 8-8-5-2 more spit and polish, which put him on a collision course with me."

"Let me put this in context for you," Doyle went on. He leaned back in his chair and looked to Joey very much like a college professor about to deliver a lecture. He was comfortable. "There is a common misconception that the army is made up of a bunch of George Pattons waiting to lead millions of young men in wild charges in the name of some greater glory. While this is true to some extent—General Horatio Stockton being one example—the army is far more complex and sophisticated. Beginning in the late 1940s, a group of officers, including myself, were brought together at the Pentagon. They all had worked on the Manhattan Project."

"The atomic bomb," blurted Joey.

"Yes," Doyle responded. "Our role was to develop a scientific arm within the military. We were to plan and oversee the development of the weapons of the future.

We were collectively known as the Section for Military Applications. We soon realized that a peace-time military lacked a major ingredient for independent scientific success—sufficient brain power. It had to be dependent on civilian federal agencies for their intellectual resources. These agencies, including the Atomic Energy Commission, have been able to harness some of the best minds from the nation's universities and private laboratories for a variety of projects that have military implications. Then came the Korean War, the renewed draft, and a great opportunity for the military. Among the hundreds of thousands of draftees were whole classes of young scientists from every discipline. We were not going to turn them into cannon fodder. We harvested them and utilized them for our own work during their tours of compulsory duty. We now have Ph.D.'s in chemistry, biology, and physics, hosts of engineers—take your pick—electrical, mechanical, metallurgical and even psychologists. Many of them are right outside my door, right now, doing wondrous things."

"I am a soldier," he continued. "I detest bright, educated draftees who selfishly reject commissions and giving at least four years of service to their country. But I do understand that if I am going to make the most of them, I must coddle them, make them feel they have a special haven for study in this unit. So I permit them to ignore dress codes and military discipline while within the laboratory section of this facility. Of course, my authority does not extend to where the enlisted men live. That area was Manigrove's jurisdiction. So, you see, we were in conflict."

"Do you do any work on radiation?" asked Conrad, her voice sounding like an interested school girl.

Doyle looked at her for a moment, his sunken eyes probing hers. "I presume as the science expert of your little group, you have been briefed on the activities of the 8-8-5-2 and my background. Yes, we are doing some studies involving radioactivity. It is in affiliation with numerous other facilities throughout the nation, including Los Alamos."

Joey leaped in still trying to get under Doyle's skin. "Who needs a briefing?

"You've got a giant black water tank out on the fringe of this unit with yellow radiation symbols around it and the word 'DANGER' in five-foot letters. I could see it from the road."

"We are obliged to warn everyone to stay away. Besides, it helps security.

Soldiers who know the symbol give this place wide berth," the lieutenant colonel replied.

Now it was Laurens' turn. "If Manigrove could function only outside the laboratories, why was he given access to them?"

"Ask the general," Doyle responded. "The captain once told me he was told to take note of dress code and discipline violators within this compound and would put them on report. He would have their passes pulled, leaves canceled, that sort of thing. Once the enlisted men caught on, they began creating fake name tags. At first, it gave him fits, but then he seemed to accept this cat-and-mouse game."

Laurens then asked if the captain acted strangely in any way. The lieutenant colonel thought for a moment. "Yes, I saw him in the lab area several times after normal working hours."

"Doing what?"

"Beats me. We work around the clock here, but most of it is between 0800 and 1600 hours."

"You never asked what he was doing?"

"No, he was Stockton's man, and he held a secret clearance."

Laurens' chin jutted out. "Did he have any close friends among your scientists?"

"He was mostly a loner, though he did seem to spend time with Corporal Victor Rodney and Corporal Frank Marconi. I presume you will want to talk to them."

"Yes, sir," Joey said as he rose from his chair. "Thank you for your time, sir. We undoubtedly will have to talk to you again soon."

Laurens gave Joey a look of anger. He had wanted to continue questioning Doyle. Then he too rose from his chair. Conrad, following Laurens' lead, got up and thanked the lieutenant colonel for his time. They got their passes stamped by Gorgeous and stepped into a fading sunset.

"Why did you cut me short?" Laurens demanded as they walked to the gate.

"I want to give him some time to think about us. He has got to know that this is about more than Manigrove's death. And I don't think he is telling us all he knows."

Joey then changed the subject. "By the way, thanks for following me in here.

Doyle was about to have me thrown in the stockade until you arrived."

"Thank General Stockton. We were starting to go through the personnel records when he walked in and suggested that we go over to the unit. He figured Doyle might get nasty with you, an enlisted man, and civilian backup would help," Laurens answered.

As they walked toward their car, Joey got the feeling that someone was behind them. He suddenly turned and thought he saw one of Doyle's guards quickly fall in with a squad of marching soldiers.

8

ꓘWELVE ꓘNGꓤY MEN

It was not yet 4:00 p.m. (1600 hours Fort Knox time), and Joey had a stop to make. He suggested Conrad and Laurens spend the rest of their day going through 8-8-5-2 personnel records. "Take your car back to the motel," he said. "Don't worry about me. I'll ask General Stockton for a car out of the motor pool."

"Will we see you tonight?" Conrad asked.

"Probably not," Joey answered. "Have a good dinner on the taxpayers. I'll catch you for breakfast at the motel, say 9:00 a.m.? We'll brief each other then."

"Can you tell us where you are going?" asked Laurens.

"Tomorrow, breakfast," Joey replied. He had learned it was best to give information on a need to know basis. The agents would need to know only if Joey found something relevant.

The FBI agents shrugged reluctant acceptance as they marched in step back to the general's office.

Joey had wanted to meet State Police Detective Sergeant Mike Thiess and had called him from his motel room before leaving for Fort Knox. Thiess suggested they meet at his office and then maybe get some dinner and a drink. That sounded fine. And by nearly 5:00 p.m., Joey was shaking hands with a grizzly bear of a man in a gray suit. His tie was a flourish of colors that nearly blinded Klugman. He instantly liked Thiess and was suddenly embarrassed that he was in uniform while Thiess was in the plain clothes of an investigator.

"Since this was my first day at Fort Knox, and I had to meet the commanding general, I thought I should show up in uniform," Joey said.

Thiess laughed. "Hey, I know all about making first impressions. I wore your uniform for quite a while myself. And I'm proud to shake the hand of a man who earned a Silver Star," the policeman said, looking at Joey's decorations. "I won one myself. Maybe we'll talk about it over supper," he added.

But first, Joey wanted to go over the state police file on Manigrove's death.

Thiess already had it on his desk. Together, they went over photographs of the captain's broken body. Thiess pointed out that there were no skid marks, no evidence that the driver attempted to stop. No evidence how Manigrove could have got to where he was found by himself. "It was just wham, slam, dual tire marks across the chest. I think the victim was already dead when he was driven here and run over while he was flat on the ground," the detective said. "Plus, there was little blood at the scene, and most of that was inside the body, where it was already pooling."

Joey agreed Manigrove was killed someplace else. "I wouldn't be surprised if those tire marks match the treads of some truck in the Knox motor pool."

"Then there was some other odd stuff," the detective continued. "The victim had three fingers broken on each hand. Unlikely that a truck would have caused those parallel kinds of injury. My coroner says his fingers were likely smashed by some blunt instrument. His guess was a hammer. Somebody systematically broke his fingers. He also had a couple of odd burn marks on his neck."

"Cigarette?" Joey guessed.

Theiss nodded. "Coroner found some traces of tobacco in the burns. Someone was having real fun."

"So, he was tortured and killed someplace else and dropped on the side of the road," Joey said. "And whoever did this must have been dumb enough to believe the local cops would think it was a hit and run."

"Lot of you Northern boys think we're all a bunch of stupid rednecks down here, ready to swallow any old story," Theiss said, chuckling and smacking his thigh.

The lawmen agreed that Manigrove must have been tortured to give up some information. But what? What did he know that was so valuable to his killers? And did he tell them what they wanted to know before he died?

"Now, I know this guy worked for some secret unit at Knox, and that's why my boss has been getting all kinds of Washington heat about solving this case as quick as possible. And that's why a CID hotshot was sent down to help us yokels out.

So, you tell me, what was this guy doing? Selling military secrets?"

"I'll be honest with you. I don't know," Joey replied. "All I can tell you is that you are right. Manigrove was working for a secret unit. I don't know if he was selling secrets or just got some guys pissed off at a poker game. I'm just starting my investigation on the base. What I suggest is that you concentrate on whatever the captain's civilian contacts were. I will work Knox."

Joey then added: "I'd love to know his movements outside the fort. Did he go to Louisville? Elizabethtown? Did he have a girlfriend? Did he . . . "

"Whoa!" Theiss cut him off. "Now, you are walking on my turf."

"Sorry," Joey replied. "You do your end. I'll do mine. Now, how about some dinner on my hotshot CID expense account?"

Theiss quickly agreed, and they were off in the detective's unmarked police car for *The Twelve Angry Men.*

"This is a place you have to see to believe," said Theiss as they drove. "It's like one of those places you see in Manhattan, like Maxwell's Plum."

"I've never been there," Joey replied, "too rich for my blood."

"C'mon, boy. With that kind of accent and you have never been to one of those swank East Side pubs and pick-up joints?"

"I've got the accent, but not the money. I just draw a master sergeant's pay." Klugman answered.

"How come a hick like you seems to know about them?"

"You take me for just another Kentucky hillbilly, wearing jeans and dancin' the Texas Two-Step," Theiss said and laughed. "It was the end of World War II, and this poor, old wounded G.I. was discharged in New York City. I had a pocket full of money and a train ticket back to Louville," he continued, using the local way of saying his home town. "Now what's a 21-year-old, horny guy going to do? I hailed a cab and told the driver to take me to one of those hot places New York was famous for. He dropped me at Maxwell's Plum. The rest is just sordid history about a fool and his money."

By the time Theiss had stopped talking, they had reached *The Twelve Angry Men*. A valet rushed to the curb, gave the detective a ticket and drove off.

They entered a short corridor of dark Spanish tile that opened into a long dimly lit room. Elvis Presley was blaring from several speakers. To the right, Joey saw a bar that ran nearly the length of the room. It had a belt of brass trim that stood out sharply from the dark maroon material that covered the rest of it. Brass spittoons dotted the floor strategically near the lengthy footrest. Some appeared to have been used. A huge mirror ran from behind the endless bottles of high-end liquor to a black ceiling. Short backed patrons' stools were done in a plush maroon material. The bartenders looked like recently retired wrestlers, each scowling menacingly at the customers. The customers seemed to enjoy their glare.

"There's a dozen of them," Theiss whispered. "That's where they got the name for this place. The clientele eats it up. Big, tough guys who take their orders and never hurt them. The place has a couple of bouncers to handle the rowdies. The bartenders just tend bar. I've checked them out. No records. But they're all connected to what you folks call the Mafia. Through family, through pals, through debts to loan sharks. One of them even is going steady with a mob hooker. My bet is they make personal collections from people who owe the wrong people."

"Nice place you take me for dinner," Joey responded.

"It may be mob run, but the steaks are great, and some of the prettiest women in Louville hang out here," Theiss said. "Same as in New York."

"Table for two?" asked a dark-haired woman who had suddenly appeared.

"Not too close to the band, Millie," the detective said.

The woman smiled a soft, knowing smile and started to escort them toward the restaurant, which formed a T with the bar. Half way down Joey suddenly halted. "Holy shit," he said loud enough to turn Theiss around. There, at the bar stood Tony Villano dressed in a gray, sharkskin suit. A thick gold chain glittered from around his neck in the subdued light. He was massaging the shoulders of Lieutenant Gorgeous.

9

GORGEOUS TROUBLE

"What was that about?" asked Theiss.

"I know two people at the bar," Joey answered. "The short guy in the fancy suit and the gorgeous broad he is with." Joey quickly explained how he had met the two.

Tony Villano had been with him on the Han River in Korea when the Chinese staged a massive night attack. The actual assault was preceded by an artillery bombardment that turned the ground into a thousand volcanoes, spewing dirt and rocks, and hurling bodies into the air. The air had become something Joey had never known before. It was a living fog enveloping him in its thick, oily, thunderous dust. It stung his skin and burned his nose with pungent drops of cordite. It resonated with every thump of death.

With a shudder, Joey remembered how he strained to see just ten feet ahead of him. He could hear the splash of oars in the water. He could hear men speaking Chinese through the din of hell.

Blindly, he hurled a hand grenade in the direction of the sound. It gave off a small flash followed by a scream of pain. Good God, they were that close.

Crouching in his fighting hole, he hurled a second grenade, then a third. Then he felt thumps, small clots of dirt jumped up. They were firing at him. Fortunately, they couldn't see any better than he could.

"I was squad leader. My platoon was dug in just beyond the river's edge," Joey recalled. "We'd dug a pretty deep trench and put up a few bunkers. Mostly, we hid in our fighting holes just beyond the trench. The shelling almost filled in the trench and smashed the bunkers. I decided to see how my men were doing. I crawled along what was left of the trench and came face to face with a Chinese soldier. I tried to shoot him, but my M-I jammed, so I smashed him in the head with my rifle butt. He wore a soft, winter cap, and I could see blood seep through it. I hit him again, and he stopped moving. Funny, I wasn't scared anymore. I didn't even think that I just killed a human being who I actually saw and touched. I was moving along numb. I was fighting for my life."

Joey stopped. That night came back to life for him. He shuddered. Theiss recognized what his companion was going through. He had felt the horrors of the infantryman's war, not once but twice. "Hey," the detective said, "You like bourbon?" Joey nodded yes.

"You can talk about it or not talk about it," he said. "I only need to know what this has to do with Tony Villano, that is if he has any bearing on this case. Otherwise, let's bury the whole thing and get a couple of steaks."

Joey nodded again and took a sip of the bourbon a waiter had quietly placed before him. "Tony was in my squad, a sniper. He seemed to enjoy his work picking off guys with an old Springfield Rifle equipped with a scope. Some thought he was kind of a ghoul for enjoying this personal killing. But we sort of bonded, both being from New York. They used to call him 'The Skinny Guinea' and me 'The Jew Bastard.' It made us closer."

Joey sensed Theiss squirm a bit at the terms. Maybe Southerners think slurs come only in black and white, he thought.

"Well, I'm crawling along this ditch, and I come across one of my men with half his head gone. He was carrying a BAR—a Browning Automatic Rifle— and a bunch of magazines. I grabbed it and the ammo and followed a commo wire—a telephone wire—and suddenly I see a bunch of Chinese and Tony Villano. He is firing a carbine and is the only one between them and the command post. Tony goes down. And one of the Chinese starts to finish him with a knife. I fire the BAR, and the Chinese guy falls. I sort of do a half turn firing. A bunch more of them drop. I get to Tony's side and start dragging him back to the CP—the command post. I guess I'm doing a John Wayne thing. Reloading, shooting, dragging Villano. Something slams through my flak jacket and something else whacks my right leg from under me, and I go down next to Tony. I'm lying there moaning, when he whispers in my ear, 'If you don't fire that fucking BAR, I will.' But he is half dead, and I am not much better. I get off some more rounds lying on my belly. I know the Chinese are rushing past me. Then, I hear one of our .50 caliber machine guns open up over my head. I bury my face in the dirt. And then it is over. No more Chinese, no more shooting. So, I try to crawl, dragging Villano, who I thought had probably bled to death, toward the CP. Then I heard a voice say, 'It's okay. We got him. You relax.'

"And that's the last time I saw Tony until today. He was training troops at Fort Knox."

Theiss threw his right hand over Joey's left shoulder. "You are the man I want with me the next time Uncle Sam puts me in a foxhole. And by the way, we old World War II guys had BARs and commo wire and CPs and M-1 rifles. They took away our muskets before sending us overseas." He laughed. He was not much older than Joey.

"Waiter, two more bourbons, two shrimp cocktails and two filet mignons, just a touch pink inside," the detective said. "I'm thankful you are still around to share this food and drink with me. But what has Tony Villano to do with our investigation?"

"The girl," Joey answered. "Lieutenant Gorgeous over there, getting massaged by Tony is light Colonel Doyle's personal aide."

Theiss's eyes widened with understanding. "Got the picture . . .I also think they got our picture. I saw the girl glance our way. She is quite a looker." As the detective finished, Tony Villano rose from his stool and walked toward their table. Lieutenant Gorgeous chatted with one of the bartenders at *The Twelve Angry Men.*

Tony approached more with a swagger than a walk. He knew he was the best-dressed man in the joint and had the prettiest girl. "Hey, soldier boy, don't you ever get out of those army duds?" he asked, not expecting an answer. "Look at me. Great suit, thick, pure gold chain, top quality leather shoes and the best looking broad in the house. You know what? Why don't we meet tomorrow, and I'll get you some great civvies and introduce you to some girls almost as good as mine?"

"I might take you up on that, but I pay my own way."

"You may have a couple of rockers on me, but army pay gets what your people call 'bupkis,'" Tony answered with a laugh.

Joey smiled.

Theiss mouthed: "What's a bupkis?"

"It's not a thing. It's a Yiddish word roughly meaning something that is worth almost nothing," Joey answered.

"Well, that's a good description of army pay," Theiss said.

Tony gave Theiss an inquiring look.

"Oh, this is Mike Theiss," said Joey. "He's with the Kentucky State Police. He's giving me some help with that captain's killing."

Tony and Theiss shook hands, sizing each other up. Each was not sure he liked what he saw. "Why don't you join us for a drink?" the detective asked. "And, of course, bring over your lovely lady friend."

"She's a little shy," Villano replied as he pulled a chair to the table. "After all, Joey is CID, and she is consorting with an enlisted man, which is a no-no."

"I swear I won't turn her in for consorting," Joey said with a laugh. But she was more tough than shy when I met her today," Joey said. "Blew me right off. Wouldn't even give me her name. So, how'd you get to know Lieutenant Colonel Doyle's personal aide, and how *well* do you know her?" Joey asked emphasizing the *well* with a wink.

"Well enough," Tony replied with a wink of his own. "Meeting her was just dumb luck. She's shopping at the Post Exchange. I say hi. She says hi. Turns out we are both from President Street in Brooklyn. One thing leads to another. We are instant soul mates."

Tony asked the waiter for Crown Royal on the rocks and signaled Gorgeous to come over. She hesitated but then walked to the table. She reminded Joey of one of those sleek sailboats that slice effortlessly through the water—all curves and taut sails.

"Carmela, I know you didn't hit it off so well with Joey earlier today, but he is the guy who saved me from a thousand Chinks in Korea. Cut him some slack." Tony then turned toward Theiss. Mike Theiss. "He is with the Kentucky State Police. He is helping Joey with the murder of that captain from your place."

Lieutenant Gorgeous smiled an angel's smile. "Charmed," she said as Theiss brought another chair to the table. "You really flipped out the colonel, especially when those FBI people showed up. You must have some juice for a master sergeant."

"Not me, the case," Joey responded.

Theiss looked surprised. "FBI? You didn't tell me anything about the FBI," he said turning to Joey.

"Sorry," Joey said sheepishly. "I'll fill you in later."

"You better," the detective answered, a note of irritation in his voice.

"Hey, I'm sorry. I didn't mean to start something," said Lieutenant Gorgeous, smiling her wondrous smile.

"It's okay, Carmela," Joey said. "Mike and I will kiss and make up. You got a last name?"

"Yes, why do you want to know?"

"Because if you ever break up with Tony, I want to take you home to Momma,"

"Momma may not like it. It's Fortunato, Carmela Fortunato." Joey preferred to think of her as Lieutenant Gorgeous.

"Hey, this guy is already cutting in on me," Tony said laughing. "I owe you, but there are limits, Joey. There are limits."

They all laughed. Gorgeous ordered a glass of wine, and after a few minutes of small talk, she and Tony returned to their place at the bar.

"Damn," Theiss said. "She walked off with that glass of wine. I already slipped his whiskey glass in my pocket. His fingerprints will be a start. Now what the hell is this with the FBI?"

As they ate their steaks, Joey explained that because some secret military information was leaked that could have come from Manigrove's unit, the FBI had attached a couple of specialists to him to handle the technical questions and help out.

"That's fine," said Theiss. "But let's not play any more games. You put all your cards on the table, and I'll do the same."

After coffee, they drove back to State Police Headquarters. They would call each other with any new information.

Joey climbed into his motor pool car and headed back toward his motel. As he reached a stretch of empty road, a sedan that had been following suddenly passed and cut in front of him. It screeched sharply to a halt, forcing Joey to slam on his breaks and stop. "You some kind of nut?" he yelled out the window. Then he saw several men pile out of the sedan.

Joey put his car in reverse, but another sedan was blocking the road behind him, and big men were getting out of that vehicle as well. He opened the door and began to sprint toward a nearby woods. But he was cut off.

They formed a circle around him. Some were carrying tire irons. The circle began to close, and Joey realized that they looked familiar. They were some of the bartenders from *The Twelve Angry Men*. One of them threw a massive fist at Joey's head. Joey ducked and countered with a hard left that made his attacker grunt. Then something hard hit him in the ribs. Someone kicked his legs out from under him, and he went down. He put his hands over his head as the pummeling continued. He was going unconscious when suddenly his attackers stopped. He was vaguely aware that there was fighting all around him. He had a flashback to that night on the Han River.

The scuffling ended with the squeal of tires. Big hands were pulling Joey to his feet. "Sorry, we didn't get here faster, Sergeant," a voice said.

Things were coming back. "I know you," Joey managed. "You were one of the guards who took me to Doyle's office. The guy from Pusan."

"I'm one of General Stockton's men, slipped into Doyle's unit. The general thought you might need some backup. When my partner and I saw those sedans following you from the night club, we called for reinforcements. This is all unofficial of course. General wants it that way." The soldier turned and left.

Joey was trying to piece it all together as he resumed his drive to the motel.

Thugs from *The Twelve Angry Men* were sent to beat him up, probably to send him a message. But what message? That this was mob business? To get off the Manigrove case? They should know better. Then there was General Stockton. Why is he having me followed? It had become a very confusing, painful night.

When Joey got to his motel room, he fell asleep almost instantly.

10

SPIES AND SPOOKS

breakfast was a painful affair. All the places on Joey's body that had been struck cried out for individual attention. It hurt him to stand, but then it hurt him to sit. And then there would be the explanation.

"My God, what happened to you?" Anita Conrad asked as Joey entered the small but clean restaurant connected to the motel. The waitress was looking at Joey and clearly thinking the same thing. His face bore the scrapes of being rubbed against gravel. Mark Laurens examined him more analytically. "This have anything to do with our investigation or were you just out having some fun last night?"

Joey appreciated Laurens' pointedness. Maybe good old boys got into fights just for the fun of it. He explained what had happened as he carefully sipped hot coffee. He'd contacted the Kentucky State Police investigator who was handling the Manigrove case. The investigator took him to a mob-run nightclub, where he bumped into a guy he had known in Korea, a sniper named Tony Villano. He had seen him earlier in the day when he was working as a drill instructor. The guy had always claimed he was connected, but most of the men in the unit bragged about one thing or another. Nobody took it seriously. But the most shocking part was that he was sitting at the bar in an expensive suit massaging the shoulders of Lieutenant Colonel Doyle's aide.

"Tony came to the table. Then the girl came over. We chatted for a few minutes and then they went back to the bar. After dinner, the detective drove me to my car, and I was ambushed on the way here. Two cars, one cut me off, and the other stopped me from backing up. Men I recognized from the bar jumped out and began wailing on me. Then a bunch of other guys showed up and began wailing on the thugs wailing on me. Everybody scrambles off, except one of the good guys, who tells me they have been ordered by General Stockton to watch me and my back."

"You had yourself quite an evening," Laurens said. "But I'm not sure of the meaning. You have an old buddy, who may or may not be a mobster, whose girlfriend is Doyle's aide. Maybe that's just coincidence. Besides, neither one seems to be doing anything wrong."

"I had the same thoughts," Joey responded. "But then the twelve angry bartenders did a dance on me—bartenders who the state police think are the collection agents for the mob. My old buddy and his girlfriend are cozy with the bartenders during the whole time I was in the restaurant. So, we have mob enforcers sending me a message, maybe from my buddy, Tony, and his girl."

"So, what's the message?" Laurens asked.

"My guess is that I was being told that Mani-grove was somehow linked to the mob, and what happened to him could happen to me. I'm interfering in mob business," Joey said.

"They could have killed you last night," Anita Conrad said.

"Not intentionally," answered Joey. "Mobsters don't kill law enforcement people, except if there is no other solution. One solution was a not-so-polite beating."

Joey found that his jaw hurt when he tried to bite down on a piece of toast, but he could swallow the scrambled eggs he had ordered if he didn't open his mouth too wide. Giving up on food, he asked, "What have you found out at your end?"

Conrad smiled a warm smile. "Like you, we found some interesting things but no smoking guns."

She and Laurens had spent the entire afternoon, going through the personnel files of the 8-8-5-2. As Lieutenant Colonel Doyle had told them, this unit could have served as the research and development team for General Electric or IBM. It was studded with Ph.D.'s from different disciplines, most in the hard sciences. Roughly half the scientists were draftees. The rest were officers who took commissions as a way to pay off education loans. All were in their mid-twenties to early 30s. The support staff was mostly regular army, people who had enlisted for patriotism or were looking for a career with a pension.

"There were a couple of people we flagged," Conrad said. "One was a nuclear physicist named Jeffrey Wade. Though he was cleared for secret work, his file goes back no farther than his college years and graduate work. According to the records, he had no childhood, no high school, no religious affiliations. He just seemed to have popped up—a full-blown genius. So we made a few phone calls to FBI headquarters and asked them to dig around. Officially, they ran into a big, red flag. Unofficially, he is a CIA makeover. This Jeffrey Wade was brought into this world as Gregor Walensky, son of Boris Walensky, once one of the Soviet Union's leading physicists."

"Boris was purged for ideological differences—he defended geneticists who favored biology over the environment. In Soviet theology, the environment is considered the primary source of all change. Plus, he was Jewish and Jews were considered inherent traitors. With the help of the Central Intelligence Agency, Boris and his wife and child defected. The CIA brought him to this country. The family was given a new identity. Boris, we believe, is a professor at some university somewhere. Son, Jeffrey, after earning a Ph.D. in biophysics, was drafted and wound up here," Conrad concluded.

Laurens picked up the briefing. "Now we come to a horse of a very different color—Corporal Victor Rodney. Rodney is an electrical engineer, graduate of MIT, an inveterate horse player and gambler. Arrested a couple of times for participating in illegal card games but no convictions. Comes from a wealthy family that seems to have disowned him."

"Anything about a Corporal Marconi?" Joey asked.

"Routine. A graduate of Brooklyn Polytechnic Institute, an electrical engineer. Eagle Scout, highest honors from Brooklyn Technical High School. Pretty much a choir boy. Parents came over from Italy, ran a candy and newspaper store in Brooklyn. He was drafted after graduation and assigned to the 8-8-5-2."

"How about Carmela Fortunato?"

"She's a very attractive woman," said Laurens.

"I knew there was something human about you, Frank," quipped Joey.

"Men," exclaimed Anita Conrad. "See a pretty woman, and you think with those compasses between your legs."

"Whee," answered Joey. "I sense a female cat with large claws."

Anita reddened. "Sorry," she said. "But pretty women have a way of clouding men's minds."

"Okay, back to business. What about Carmela?" Joey replied.

Laurens slipped back into his hard-eyed role. "She is a study in contrasts. She is the niece of one Anthony Lanteri, a Mafia boss who resides in Brooklyn, New York. He specializes in narcotics, loan-sharking, prostitution and the sale of all kinds of contraband, from firearms to cigarettes. His enemies have been found dead in the trunks of stolen cars or floating in the Hudson River or they conveniently disappear.

"Carmela seems not to have been a part of her uncle's operations, though on a family level they are very close. Lots of dinners at her mother's home; lots of family vacations in the Italian section of the Catskills.

"But for the young lady, no convictions, no arrests. Nothing. She was an honors student in high school, went on to New York University, where she got a degree in business. She went to work for the Manhattan accounting firm of Mazzi, Levy, and Barnswell. After three months, she quit and joined the Women's Army Corps. She told her recruiter that she couldn't get anywhere in the accounting company because she was a woman and would have better opportunities in the army. She got top scores in everything from marksmanship to stenography and was commissioned a second lieutenant in 90 days. She got assigned to the 8-8-5-2 because Lieutenant Colonel Doyle sent out a call for an aide with brains enough to deal with the unit's work and its unique personnel.

"One other thing, that Mazzi firm keeps the books for Lanteri's legitimate businesses. We believe dirty money is laundered through these businesses but have never been able to prove it."

The investigators agreed they had found a number of interesting characters, all of whom knew Manigrove but none of whom had a discernable reason to kill him. They would have to start examining the connections between the captain and these characters. Conrad and Laurens would interview the newly minted Jeffrey Wade. Joey would talk to Corporals Vincent Rodney and Frank Marconi.

Since they now had two cars, they would rendezvous in the parking lot that fronted the general's office and walk to the 8-8-5-2.

"You guys find a good restaurant?" Joey asked as they rose to leave.

"No, we ate in," Anita Conrad responded.

"Damn. Did Laurens score?" thought Joey with a touch of envy.

11

JOEY'S STORY

Joey walked back to his motel room keeping pace with the two FBI agents. But his body resented every step. After being kicked and punched and smacked with tire irons, it deserved rest.

He fumbled with his key for a moment before entering his neat, little room. The myriad of pink and red flowers that designed the yellow bedspread seemed too nice, too sweet, too peaceful for the pain that haunted his ribs. He flopped down heavily on the bed and rested. He would stay there for a few minutes to gather his strength.

As the pain drained into the mattress, Joey looked up at what had at first appeared as a smooth white ceiling. Then, like in a reversed image, he noticed that the white was divided by thin, long spider leg cracks that crawled out from corners into the white abyss. Nothing is as it seems as first. His life had been like that. He had been shaped for peace, yet he became a warrior. It was the Monopoly fight that changed him, that taught him his parents' way only led to more trouble.

Years ago, he had stared up at a similar ceiling with similar spider leg cracks in the living room of his family's tight, little apartment in Queens, New York. At night, its pull-out couch served as his bed. He would lie there wide awake looking up at the ceiling with its lacy legs and wonder if it could tell him how his life would be. He knew he didn't want to drive a laundry truck, like his father. But not wanting isn't the same as wanting.

The wanting was missing. Better to stare up at the white, spider cracked ceiling and hope that like some great multi-armed god, it would pull him from his bed, embrace him and say: "Love me, swear allegiance to me, and I will tell you what to be." But the ceiling remained mute and uncaring. Joey would have to find his own way.

Other people's lives weren't that confused. His cousin, Jeremy's life, had immediate purpose. Jeremy always had wanted to be a doctor, since they were four years old and played together on their tenement's fire escape. He always wore a toy stethoscope around his neck, a gift from his mother. "My son will be a doctor," Aunt Tillie would announce proudly. And Jeremy, with all the vigor of youth propelled by a determined matriarch, was on his way to that paradigm of the modern, western Jewish mark of success—the medical degree. He went to Princeton and graduated cum laude. Columbia University's School of Medicine beckoned. Life was on automatic pilot for Jeremy and Aunt Tillie.

Several distinct levels down on that paradigm scale of American Jewish business success were dentist, lawyer, optometrist, and podiatrist. Somewhat lower were college professor, accountant, businessman, and salesman—if he made a lot of money, usually in dresses, furniture or printing. Musicians, actors, comedians, scientists, and journalists fell into a special category. Nice for the prestige but no money in it. Basically for the crazies. Rabbis? That depended on whether they had a sizable congregation. Joey's choice—professional soldier—didn't exist. It was just not a thing Jews did willingly.

Jews had learned that they usually ended up badly when it came to fighting, not because they were afraid or inept. They simply were too often outnumbered and outgunned. Biblically, they had fought the Egyptians, the Assyrians, the Babylonians, the Persians, the Romans and a variety of others with bad results. Ironically, they stood up to the Romans so well, that Rome used Jewish mercenaries to guard the limits of its far-flung empire. In more recent times, they found themselves conscripted into the armies of kings, kaisers, czars, and dictators to fight for causes they disliked in places they didn't want to be.

World War II was different for the Jews. Thousands fought in America's armed forces for what was clearly the best of causes, but almost none considered making the military a career. When the war ended, they went back to being doctors, lawyers and dress salesmen—known to insiders as being in "the rag trade."

Joey was too young for World War II and probably would have gone into one of the acceptable occupations for Jews, forever a round peg shoved into that square hole—except for the Monopoly fight.

It began with a walk through a vacant Queens lot, made up mostly of construction sand, beer cans, worn-out rubber tires and old mattresses displaying rusty springs. Joey's neighborhood was divided into ethnic enclaves. The Jews had their section, the Italians theirs and the Irish theirs. There were several no man's lands. Everybody knew them, and they were to be avoided. One was the lot that ran roughly parallel to the Long Island Rail Road tracks, ending near Union Turnpike.

Joey had stayed late at his friend Burley's house and decided to chance the shortcut across the lot to save a few minutes. He was 14 at the time and was developing the chiseled build his father once possessed. He and Burley had played Monopoly for most of the afternoon, and the Monopoly set was tucked safely under Joey's arm as he crossed the lot. Some odd-looking weeds grew in scanty patches in the sad, white soil. Clearly, the lot was a hard place. Then he saw the three Irish kids, all about his age, sitting around a fire they had built. They saw him at the same time. It was too late to run, so Joey kept on walking, head down trying to mind his own business.

"Hey, Jewish kid," the big one named Jerry yelled rising to his feet and walking up to Joey. "We need your Monopoly money for our fire, or it will go out, maybe the board too. And with one swift motion, he knocked the Monopoly box out from under Joey's arm. A strong piece of cord held the box together, but a few pieces of the game's money fell out. Jerry immediately seized the yellow and green pieces of paper. "Want them back, Jew boy?" he asked. Without waiting for an answer, he turned and fed them to the fire.

Joey was caught between anger and terror. Jewish elders had advised the young to avoid confrontations. Better to take a little name calling than suffer cuts and bruises. "Stop!" Joey screamed. Jerry just laughed and went to pick up the box. It was at that point that Joey's terror turned to rage. He owned precious few things in this world and the Monopoly set was one of them. He closed his right hand into a hard ball and swung with a blind fury. He felt a crunching sound as his fist smashed into Jerry's nose. Blood splattered back on Joey's face. He didn't care. He swung his left hand, bouncing it off Jerry's head and toppling him backward. He landed with a scream on top of the fire.

The other two boys froze momentarily in shock. Then they got to their feet and charged Joey. He barely felt himself get thrown to the ground, and he didn't feel the kick to his ribs until much later. As he struggled to his feet, one of the boys hit him hard in the eye, but Joey's rage carried him beyond pain. He hit back, his right fist landing with a thud on the chest of one boy. The other boy punched Joey in the back. Joey dropped to his knees but popped back up, swinging both hands. His right hand caught one of them on the side of the face. "He won't stay down!" yelled one of his attackers, giving Joey a sharp kick. Joey staggered. He had no feeling in his left leg. He was about to go down again.

But he and the others became aware that Jerry was screaming. "Get me home. Get me home. I can't see, I'm burned, and my nose is broken. Oh, Jesus, it's broken." His companions backed away from Joey. Each grabbed an arm and walked Jerry toward the group of apartments that marked the Irish ghetto. They looked back long enough to give Joey the finger.

Joey dropped to his knees and picked up the crushed box that still contained most of his Monopoly set. He was crying. The rage had left him, and he could feel the pain. But he still had his Monopoly set. He had fought, and he had won. And it changed him. He found something he could do well. He could fight. Maybe he would become a professional fighter like Max Baer or Slapsy Maxie Rosenbloom or Barney Ross. Or maybe he would become a professional soldier and fight for his country.

He tried fighting for a while at a local gym. He became good enough to enter a Golden Gloves tournament. His first opponent was fast but couldn't hurt him. Joey knocked him down twice in the third round and was declared the winner. His second foe caught him with a left hook to the stomach that nearly lifted Joey off his feet. He was strong but very slow. Joey jabbed and danced and won a decision. In his third fight, his challenger hit harder and moved faster than Joey, who just managed to stay on his feet as the fight ended. "There are fighters who are both faster than me and stronger than me," Joey thought. "Professional soldiering would make more sense."

It took several years after he had made his decision for Joey to gather the courage to tell his parents. It was just before his graduation from high school. His mother fell heavily into a chair. His father turned ashen and scratched unthinkingly at the old scar on his right leg. He walked back and forth in the apartment's living room for a few moments before saying anything. Joey knew that a lot of young men had died in the recently concluded Second World War. He expected that argument.

Then Max Klugman began: "Your mother and I were born in this little town in the Austro-Hungarian Empire called Stanislaw. Town? I should say little city with a bunch of farms around it. My father was a merchant and a woodworker of considerable skill, so we lived in the city part. Everything was more or less okay until 1914 when the Empire joined with Germany to fight England, France, Italy, and Russia."

"Pop, I know all about the First World War, we studied it in school," Joey interrupted.

"What I'm telling you now isn't in the history books. It's what happened to me and your grandfather," Max Klugman said. "I never told you this stuff, but I think now is the time you should learn a little about your family history. I was just 17. Your grandfather, Avram Klugman, was forty, a big, powerful, handsome man with a dark beard. The Empire drafted him and me into the army. We trained together for a few weeks, and then they separated us. My father's unit went to support the Germans in the Ardennes Forest in France. My mother got a few letters from him describing his life. They fought in deep trenches filled with water fouled by human waste. Dead bodies floated in the water as well. The shelling went on all the time, day and night." Max paused. "Then the letters stopped."

"I was sent to the Italian Alps. I was in the cavalry and rode a horse when the ground was level. When we finally got high enough to where the Italians were, we couldn't ride our horses. But that was okay because we were starving. So we shot the horses and ate them."

"Now I had nothing against the Italians. In fact, I could never remember meeting one until we climbed into their mountains. There I could see them. They had fur coats and rifles, and they were shooting at us. I was scared I was going to die up there in their mountains, so I shot back. We all shot back. Everybody was digging ditches and shooting up at those flashes coming from holes on the mountainside.

When both sides finally got dug in, we would take turns charging at each other. First would come the artillery barrage, then the command to go forward, and we would leap up and run up the mountain. Then the machine guns would open up, killing and wounding many of us. The survivors would fall back into their trenches and cry for our friends lying out there. Then came the Italians' turn. The barrage, the charge, the dead falling on our barbed wire. Except one time an Italian soldier got so close to me, I could see his large eyes. I thought I saw fear, anger, desperation in those eyes. Then he threw a hand grenade at me. I ran. Then I felt myself flying. I don't remember when I woke up, but a medic was saying, 'You'll be okay. You won't lose your leg.' I looked down at my right leg, and a big chunk of metal was sticking out of it."

Max suddenly pulled up his right pants leg. "Look, boy. Look at one of the effects of war. I still have got a piece of the shrapnel in me." Joey stared at the jagged, reddish scar that ran down his father's right calf. He had seen it before but never asked Max how he got it. Now, Joey slowly ran his hand along the scar.

"The doctors decided the best thing to do was leave some of the metal in. It was too close to an artery. The good part in all this was that I got to go to a hospital where I ate real food." Max Klugman paused, summoning up images from the past. "Your grandmother would visit and bring me kosher meals, which the way she made them were delicious. I couldn't tell her about eating horses. Jews aren't supposed to eat horses."

"Does it still hurt?" Joey asked, pointing at the scar.

"It still hurts, especially when the weather changes," Max answered.

"And grandpa?" Joey asked.

"One day, my mother told me, some men in spectacular uniforms filled with gold braid came to her door and gave her box with an Iron Cross in it, and told her that her husband was a hero, that he had died bravely, leading a charge against the enemy. There would be no body returning. He was blown to pieces."

"In the end, the Austro-Hungarian Empire was no more, and I was on my way to America. I met your mother, Rebecca, on the same ship that took me to this new country. We fell in love. We married. We had you, who has been forever the apple of our eyes. And now you want to chance getting yourself blown up like your grandfather," Max concluded.

The family discussion ended with an agreement. Joey would go to college, and if he still wanted to go into the military after graduation, they would not object. Joey went to Queens College of the City of New York and graduated with a comfortable B average from a school noted for its tough academic standards. It was 1952. The decision on going into the military was taken out of Joey's hands. He was drafted. As his parents wept, Joey, privately happy, went off to the bitter Korean War. He survived battles along the Han River, where he won a Silver Star and Purple Heart. He spent nearly a year recovering at Valley Forge Army Hospital. The war had ended by the time Joey was fully recovered, but he had decided to stay in the army. The adventure excited him, as well as the good feeling of hitting back.

As he lay in his motel room bed, he remembered his last confrontation with his parents. They had driven down the New Jersey Turnpike to meet Joey at Camp Kilmer. Joey was eligible for release to inactive duty.

They met in a civilian reception area. The Klugmans glowed with joy. "Our Joey is back in one piece, and he looks beautiful," his mother cried throwing her arms around him. Her tears made small black dots on his spotless uniform. Then it was his father's turn. Max hugged his son and kissed him on the cheek. "You did better than I did in Italy. You got no shrapnel to keep inside you," he said. "But why no duffel bag?

"I re-enlisted," Joey replied.

His parents looked at him in stunned silence. "You are joking," his father finally said, unbelieving. "I just got you set up with a fine job in the dress industry. Your cousin, Larry, got it for you. Fifty thousand a year once you get into the swing of things. It's with Ellie Louise, a hot name in the business."

"Pop, I'm going to serve four more years in the army," Joey replied. "I'll see after that."

"You almost got killed. Wasn't that enough?" Max asked.

"I love being a professional soldier. I signed the papers. It's done. Besides, I'm not going back into a combat unit. I'm going into the Criminal Investigation Division. I'm going to be a detective."

"You did this to spite us?" his mother asked. "You did this to show the goyim how tough a Jew can be?"

"No, Momma. I did this because I love my country. I love the adventure, and I am very good at what I do."

12

A TALK WITH TONY

The banging on his door brought Joey to his feet. "Yeah," he shouted. "It's Anita, you okay? I'm a doctor, remember?"

"I'm a little shaky, but I'm okay," Joey responded, not sure that he meant it. "I just need a few more minutes. I'll leave a message at the general's office as to where we can meet up."

"Sure," Anita responded. "Just remember. We are the cavalry. We are great at rescuing people."

Joey laughed and thanked her. "And my best to Mr. Laurens. I hope you both had a wonderful night." He heard her footsteps move away from his door.

Just then the phone rang. "Hey, this is Mike, Mike Theiss. You sleeping late on the job, boy," the detective said. "It's near on to 10 o'clock."

"I had a headache," Joey managed.

"Can't take the booze, huh?" the detective chuckled.

"Something like that," Joey responded choosing not to go into a long explanation until he met with Theiss.

"Those prints I took of your friend told a real story," the detective said. "He told you he was a member of the mob? Well, that wasn't bullshit. He is a member in very good standing. Before he took to killing North Koreans and Chinese, he got some basic training killing good, old fashioned Americans. Of course, the NY cops couldn't prove it. But they got him for some minor stuff, running numbers, burglary, assault with a hammer on a union boss. That was pleaded down. No jail time, just probation. He is what they call a soldier in the Lanteri crime family."

"That makes two," Joey answered. "His girlfriend, Lieutenant Gorgeous, Carmela Fortunato, I should say, is Lanteri's niece."

"Wow," Theiss replied. "Have they come together for love or money?"

"My bet is both," said Joey. "And it has to do somehow with the 8-8-5-2."

Theiss said he would check with the Louisville police to see if they had heard any word on the street about something coming in from Fort Knox or going out to the fort.

Joey would do the same on the base. His plan was to talk to two of the laboratory enlisted men Manigrove had spent time with.

Joey decided to wear his uniform again. He might be more intimidating to the two draftee corporals he planned to question. They had been pushed around by enough sergeants to make them think push-ups whenever one of them approached. He added one extra item—a .32 caliber pistol he strapped into an ankle holster. Of course, having one side of his face scrapped and topped by a black eye somewhat offset the tough master sergeant look he wanted to convey. But there was nothing he could do about that kind of damage.

He slid into his carpool sedan and started to pull out of the parking lot when a familiar voice from the back seat said; "Turn right not left. There is a little cafe just down the road where we can sit and talk."

"You're not going to shoot me in the head and dump me off the side of the road?" Joey asked.

"Don't be a jerk. It's not like that at all, at least not with you," answered Tony Villano. He was dressed in his army fatigues. He looked worn and tired.

As they stepped from the car, Tony made a point of walking ahead of Joey. He was telling him he was no threat, just maybe a friend—or maybe not. Maybe there was a backup car with some of the bartenders from *The Twelve Angry Men* in it waiting to finish the job.

The cafe had one of those squeaking screen doors that slammed behind them so quickly it frustrated all but the swiftest flies. Those that made it in soon fell victim to the sticky fly paper strategically placed around the food making and food eating areas. A worn and skinny waitress with a smile that happily displayed her missing teeth greeted them with a greasy menu.

"Couple eggs over easy," Tony said, as he slid into a chair. "And coffee."

"Make it two coffees," said Joey.

"Nothin' else?" the waitress asked, sounding disappointed. Joey shook his head, and she headed off for the kitchen.

"Now what's this all about?" he asked, looking Tony squarely in the eyes.

"I had nothing to do with what happened to you last night. I want you to know that right off. If I had known she was setting that up, I would have stopped her—or them."

"Her? You mean Lieutenant Gorgeous?"

"Yeah, Carmela. She's gorgeous all right and a terrific fuck. But she could cut out your heart after licking your balls. And don't ever forget it."

"Look at my face. How can I forget it? And I didn't get my balls licked first. So why? Was she trying to send me a message? A message that says the mob is involved and anybody could get hurt."

"Yeah, but why beat up a cop? You kill him, they send two cops. Carmela is smart. She had a reason, and she is the boss, even when it comes to me, at least in this friggin fort. But I will tell you this: we are making money, good money."

"So, you are here to be the nice thug and offer me money or maybe a taste of Gorgeous to white-wash Manigrove's death and get out of here?"

Tony grinned. "There are always choices," he said.

"I brought you toasted rye bread," the waitress interrupted with her gap-toothed smile. She clearly was taken with Tony. He had a strong, angular face with straight, bright, white teeth. He was more manly looking than handsome.

Tony lit up. "Thanks, Frieda. I forgot to mention the toast," he answered. She smiled again. Then she turned and walked away dodging fly paper.

Tony turned serious. "I am your friend. Or maybe I'm not your friend. I haven't figured that out.

But I owe you. I owe you big time. You saved my ass. So let me give you a little payback. If you want to be in on the action, I can arrange it. The money is good," he said

Joey wrinkled his face.

"I know," Tony went on. "I didn't think so, but it was worth a try. And I know that while you would love to hump Carmela, I am not offering her to you. Besides, your type can't be bribed with pussy. Straight arrows, your type. That's why you couldn't leave me there to die that night. You fucking straight arrow."

"You would have done the same for me."

"Bullshit. I would have run as fast as my little Italian legs would take me. And I wouldn't have stopped to drag some son-of-a-bitch Jew along with me."

"I don't believe that," Joey responded.

"Believe what you like," Tony said, wiping his rye toast into egg yolk. "My thinking is Doyle put her up to the beating. She does things for Doyle. And I don't mean just army things. I don't know what he has with her. Somehow, it's part of what goes on here. But he is the only one who can tell her to do something, and she will do it."

"Like what?" asked Joey with a slight smile.

"Not what's in your filthy mind. More like getting wise-assed guys like you beat to death."

"Or shaken to death?" Tony asked

"I've said enough," the mobster answered.

Tony threw a five-dollar bill on the table, winked at Frieda and led Joey out passed the swiftly moving screen door. The last he saw of Frieda, she was clearing still living flies from the fly paper.

13

ALPHA, BETA, GAMMA

Jeffery Wade sat behind a plain desk filled with notes and scientific scribblings.

Though Laurens and Conrad had seen a picture of him, they were surprised at just how young he looked. He appeared more like a tall, slender teenager than a 23-year-old Ph.D. from MIT. His army fatigues appeared far too large for his body. When he rose to greet them, he demonstrated the physical awkwardness of boys whose coordination has not yet caught up to their growing limbs. Yet his deep brown eyes seem filled with the depth of a much older man. Conrad had the sense that Wade had seen and felt too much pain for someone so young.

"How do you do?" he said with an engaging smile.

Conrad immediately liked him.

Laurens felt neither like nor dislike for Wade. He saw a man whose physical fragility masked an inner toughness, someone who had been hardened by the events of his life—perhaps too many interrogations by the KGB and the CIA. He would be clever.

He would talk but say little. "Now he sits among more American military secrets than most federal agents see in a career," Laurens thought. "This is some kind of bad spy joke. Is he ours? Is he theirs? Do we both have him? Or does he have all of us?"

"Sergeant Wade, let me get right to the point," Laurens said aloud. "What do you know about Captain Albert Ruppert Manigrove III and his death?"

"Almost nothing and nothing," Wade replied coolly. "I do not understand why the FBI is here and talking to me about this man's death." He paused. "Unless you have reason to believe he was spying. And if so, why come to me? I am a lowly sergeant, a laboratory rat working on esoteric experiments. I prefer mind games to violence."

He was playing a mind game now, Anita thought. He suspects that we know his real identity, but he is not sure. He has been told that his old identity will never be revealed. For the CIA to do so—even to the FBI—would be a crime. But the CIA had left an opening by leaving too many gaps in Wade's background.

"I'll be straightforward with you," Conrad began. "You know you work at a secret installation, that your work here is sensitive and could affect the security of this nation. Captain Manigrove was a part of this unit and had clearance to go anywhere. So, yes, when such a person meets a violent death, we investigate. And yes, there is always the question of espionage."

"I barely knew the man," Wade responded. "So why talk to me?"

"Because we checked the files and backgrounds of all the personnel at the 8-8-5- 2, and yours doesn't make sense," Conrad continued. "Your records show no real life before your time at MIT. We checked the high school listed in your files, and it has no record of you. You gave your religious affiliation as Jewish, but when we checked all the synagogues and temples in your alleged hometown, none had or could recall a family named Wade. And Wade is such an odd name for a Jewish family, they all said they would remember it. So now I am sure you understand why we are questioning you." Anita added, "You have a slight accent, not the kind anyone born in this country would have."

Jeffrey Wade did not skip a beat. He smiled a sweet smile and said, "Okay, you have me. I was not born in this country, and my name originally was not Jeffrey Wade. I was told if such a situation as has now occurred to tell my interrogators to contact a Mathew VanBuren. I will write down his telephone number. I am sorry. I can tell you no more." With that, he scribbled a Washington, D.C., number on a notepad sheet and handed it to Conrad.

She took the sheet and tucked it away in her pocket book. "We will call Mr. VanBuren," she said.

Laurens immediately took up the questioning. "We will put off exploring your background. But we want you to talk about your contact with the captain specifically."

"We met briefly two or three times over the past few months. He mainly asked me about my work, which he clearly did not understand.

Then, once, he asked me what I knew about the work of the electrical engineering group. I told him, I knew nothing."

"Why did he ask you about the electrical engineers?" Laurens went on.

"I have no idea," Wade answered.

"What is your relationship with Lieutenant Colonel Doyle?" Anita asked.

Wade broke into a wide grin. "He is like my father. He is a great mentor to me. He has great knowledge in the field of radiation. And that is my area of expertise. That is what I study here," he said pointing in the direction of the laboratory's facilities.

"Can you be more specific about what you do?" the agent asked.

"My colleagues and I study the effects of so-called ionizing radiation on animals and plants. Before the atomic bomb, we knew very little about this phenomenon. Oh, we knew a little from studying those who painted faces of wristwatches with radium so they would glow in the dark. They began getting cancer well out of proportion to their numbers in the general population. That was in the 1920s and 30s. Then came August 6th, 1945. An atomic bomb is dropped on Hiroshima and those who did not die immediately from the heat and concussion, died days, weeks, months and years later first from radiation burns, then from radiation sickness. These illnesses came as somewhat unexpected side effects of the explosion. The bomb had released a surprising amount of radiation particles into the atmosphere. America had let a terrible genie out of its bottle. Now my colleagues and I are part of an army of scientists seeking to determine just how terrible this genie can be."

He looked across the hall from his office at a long, dark tubular machine that was aimed, like a rifle, at a cage open only on the side facing the device. "You see that machine," he said to the agents. "It works something like the x-ray machine dentists now use to look for cavities in your teeth. But this machine is much more powerful. It bombards atoms with high energy electrons. We can vary the amount of energy and the flow of electrons from the tube. We put rats in those cages and bombard them with x-rays of varying doses. We then watch for the effects on these creatures. It is never good."

Wade then explained that his laboratory also was working on the effects of alpha, beta and gamma rays as well as those of neutrons. "Am I losing you?" he asked, like some friendly teacher.

"Each Alpha particle is made up of two neutrons and two protons, quite like the nucleus of the helium atom," Anita replied. "Beta particles are electrons traveling at very high energies. Gamma and X-ray radiation consist of packets of energy called photons, like the light our eyes see. Neutrons are components of an atom's nucleus. They have no electrical charge, and once released can travel virtually unhindered through most materials."

"True," Wade replied, clapping his hands and smiling with the joy of being understood. "You have some knowledge in this area, Agent Conrad?"

"Some," she responded, not wanting to divulge her medical degree or knowledge of biophysics.

"I sense, perhaps, that you are not ordinary agents. Am I correct?"

"You can think or sense whatever you want," Laurens broke in. "What is your relationship with Carmela Fortunato?" he continued.

"None. I say hello. She says hello. She is a pretty woman. I notice her, but that is all," Wade replied.

"Does she have a personal relationship to Lieutenant Colonel Doyle?" Laurens pressed."

For the first time, Wade hesitated for just a fraction of second before replying, "Not that I know of," he said.

"Do you experiment on human beings?" Conrad asked.

Again, there was a slight hesitation. "I deal only with the subjects authorized to me by Lieutenant Colonel Doyle."

"You didn't answer my question," Conrad pressed.

"I am in the army. I do as I am told. I must refer these technical questions to my superior," he answered. Color rose in Wade's face, and his angular frame seemed to twitch inside its baggy fatigue covering.

"We'll do that," Laurens said. "And we will be back to talk some more."

Once away from the 8-8-5-2, Laurens called FBI headquarters and asked for full-time surveillance of Jeffrey Wade. "We could have another Klaus Fuchs on our hands," he told his superior.

Later, the agents called Mathew VanBuren, whose initial response was: "I'll call you back."

Twenty minutes later, an agitated Van Buren called them back. "I have spoken to your superiors. You are to leave Jeffrey Wade alone. Absolutely, no contact."

With that, he clicked off.

14

DOYLE AND WADE
A LONG TALK

They sat across the room from each other, each a time capsule reflection of the other. Francis X. Doyle, 56. Jeffrey Wade, 23, each nearly six feet three inches. Each slightly stooped from talking to those below their height and intellectual level. Each rail thin. Each awkward in motion. Each pale, though Doyle's paleness was far more a chalky white. Each sharply boned, though Doyle more so. His flesh crept tightly around hard corners, making his face a skull-like mask and his body more skeleton than flesh.

Both had eyes that carried hints of their electric intelligence. They were atomic physicists of a high order. Doyle had worked with the best of them, even before the bomb—Oppenheimer, Teller, Evans, Lawrence and all those others, those dear, dear others. He had once talked briefly with Albert Einstein on the unity in the space/time continuum.

Wade already had worked with Dr. Shields Warren, the first chief of the Atomic Energy Commission's

Division of Biology, and had attended lectures by Navy Captain C.F. Behrens, who edited the seminal medical text on the radiation era, *Atomic Medicine.*

He had heard both these men struggle with the ethical issues raised by the necessity for nuclear research and the desire for the well-being of those involved in such research. This was especially agonizing for the medical doctors who had taken an oath to do no harm.

Doyle had listened to those discussions many times. What about the overriding issues for all of humanity, he had thought? American scientists, despite Oppenheimer, had moved on to the creation of a hydrogen bomb, a weapon of so much power that if any surviving humans wished to continue fighting after a nuclear exchange, they would do so with spears and stones, according to a noted scientist. The American and Soviet leadership didn't seem to care. Only a balance of terror between the two superpowers seemed a viable option.

"The FBI visited me today," Wade said. "They said they didn't know about me, but they knew."

"And what did you tell them?" Doyle asked.

"I told them the truth," the young man replied. "But not all of it. I gave them the name of the CIA man who is my overseer for the details. He is supposed to deny them any information, but who knows? They all are members of the secret police."

"Wise," Doyle said. "Perhaps, they will think you are untouchable."

Wade smiled a sad smile. "I don't think so," he said. "One seemed to know a good deal about ionizing radiation. The other was the bulldog. Strong, hard, the bone breaker. He could work for the KGB. My sense is they are looking for spies here. They are looking for us."

Doyle shook his head as if to shed all the betrayals that had led him to this. But they hung on him like so many heavy, unbreakable chains. "It is this Manigrove thing," he said. "His killing set off all these investigations. I have attempted to create a distraction. But I don't know whether they will take the bait and hunt down those I have offered them."

Wade slapped his slender legs and laughed. "That reminds me of the old Russian story about the three men riding in a droshky. It is a cold winter. The snow is deep. Everyone and everything is hungry. And they are chased by wolves. When the wolves get too close, the two strongest throw the third man off the droshky and into the snow. While the animals feast, the two get away. Survival of the fittest," he said.

"If we are fortunate, the wolves will feast on what I have thrown them and allow us to slip away as well," Doyle answered.

Then the older man stood up and with some effort walked over to the younger. He grasped Wade's shoulders with affection. "I feel like the father who has sent his son on a very dangerous mission. Now, I want you to stop. No more meetings with your courier, no more detailed packets from me, not at least until the authorities have gone."

"I already telephoned Colonel Karpov to warn him to leave," Wade said. Seeing the apprehension on Doyle's face, he added, "I took the precaution of calling from a pay phone."

Doyle smiled. "Smart boy," he said.

Then he walked slowly around his sparse office. "I am sorry I got you into this. You and your father may pay bitterly."

"My father thinks as you do. Science is not for the U.S.S.R. or the United States. It is for humanity. These things we are finding show that everyone everywhere will suffer horrible deaths in a nuclear war. With the Hydrogen Bomb, there will be no bunkers in which to hide, no places so far away, they will be immune. The radiation will find all of us everywhere."

"Well said," Doyle replied. "Good men do bad things for good reasons. So we have given our findings and those at Los Alamos to the Soviets, not to aid them but to warn them of the devastation they will bring upon themselves as well as others should they use nuclear weapons. We are giving them knowledge and from that knowledge will come fear. And from that fear will come humanity's salvation."

Doyle then gently touched Wade's hair. "I had always wanted a son, a son who would grow up like you, follow in my footsteps then go beyond them. But that was not to be. Instead, you were bequeathed to me by, of all things, the military draft. Our minds touched. Formulas, concepts leaped into our heads. We see the future as few others can. But now I may have put you in prison. Or worse got you sent you back to Russia."

The older man thought back to that time six months ago when they sat in this very same office and talked for the first time about atomic physics and biology. He had done this routinely as new scientists were sent to him. The 8-8-5-2 was filled with Ph.D. physicists, but Doyle knew immediately there was none with a mind like Wade's. It was as if he always had lived in a world of particles, where energy and matter flickered back and forth, rearranging themselves in countless ways.

"We must look at particles as communities that function as one, like bees in a hive or ants on a mound. We must account for them and their movements statistically and with probability theory. They defy separate measurement," Doyle said.

On his part, young Wade sensed he was in the presence of someone who could come near the genius of his father. And when Doyle mentioned that he had exchanged papers with the Soviets' giant of physics, Wade, filled with pride, revealed that he was Gregor Walensky, son of the great Boris Walensky, the Nobel Prize winner in theoretical physics. He knew he could trust this man.

His father had antagonized the Kremlin with his outspoken support of genetic research, an area that was ideologically forbidden. His demands for an unfettered science ended the Politburo's patience. Boris Walensky was removed from all his scientific positions.

"Your secret clearances are withdrawn. You will be exiled with your family to Siberia, where you will continue your research and discussions with the trees and the bears," said Colonel Vladimir Karpov, a high-ranking official of the KGB, the Soviet secret police. "You have betrayed the leadership and thus the people. You have failed to see that human beings can and will be changed almost totally by their environment.

"Communism's redistribution of wealth will change every human being so they can live up to their full capacity. No one is inherently limited by his biological makeup," he lectured. "Communism will lead us all to that promised land that religionists always long for. You, being Jewish, should know all about the promised land," he told the Walensky family.

Boris Walensky knew that without his secret clearances, he could no longer talk to his fellow physicists or for that matter any scientist on the cutting edge of his profession in the Soviet Union. His career was over.

Karpov was no fool. He understood the sentence that had been handed down. It castrated Walensky intellectually. He may just as well talk with the trees. No ordinary individual could or would comprehend his thoughts. But the KGB colonel was not a cruel man. He was born to a dirt-poor peasant family that had been liberated from virtual bondage by the Communist Revolution. He had been able to rise from his humble beginnings through his bravery during World War II and his fervor for the cause of Marx and Lenin. He truly believed that Communism was the answer to a better life for all human beings.

The Walenskys were nice people, but they stood in the way of the worldwide revolution that was about to come. Regrettably, they would have to be among the broken eggs needed make Lenin's omelet—the creation of a new world order.

It was the weakness of his humanity that led Karpov to a tactical error. He allowed the elder Walensky to take his wife Rivka and his son Gregor with him to the Siberian labor camp that was to be his home. In Rivka, Boris Walensky found the courage and strength to survive their harsh surroundings. In Gregor, he had the mind that could and would understand his universal thoughts. He would have to be trained, but now there was time for that.

They were packed onto a boat with others in need of Soviet re-education for the long trip up the Lena River to Siberia. In some perverse way, it was a time-honored journey for enemies of the state. The Czars had sent many of their undesirables on this river cruise from which few returned.

The Walenskys' journey ended in Nyuya, a village built largely by ethnic Germans in 1941 after their forced removal from what had been the Soviet Union's German Autonomous Republic. A bureaucrat, not Karpov, thought it would be amusing to resettle an unwanted Jewish scientist and his family among unwanted Germans.

During the day, the Walenskys labored with the others. But at night, by a tiny fire, Boris would reveal to his son the secrets of the universe. Rivka rocked in her chair and smiled as she watched the transmission of knowledge she could never understand. It was important to know only that this communication was taking place.

Then, one night, a knock came at the door of their tiny hut. It was Jakob, an ethnic German who acted as a camp supervisor. "A fisherman is asking for you at the dock. He says he worked with you and wants to say hello. It's up to you if you want to see him," Jakob said, implying permission.

Puzzled, yet ever curious, Boris wrapped his thin jacket around him and went to the dock. There, sitting in a small deep-hulled sailboat, sat a gray-bearded man wearing a small peak cap over curly dark hair. In deep-voiced Russian, he said: "F equals Large G times Large M times small *m* divided by small *d* squared." And waited.

Boris did not know this man, but he knew the formula. "It is Isaac Newton's Universal Law of Gravity."

"How do you explain its conclusions in light of Einstein's Special Theory of Relativity?" asked the man on the boat.

Boris was about to reply when the man cut him short. "Don't bother," he said with a short laugh. "Just a little test that I was talking to the right man. Now, bring your wife and son to my boat as soon as possible. If you want to be free, don't argue. Just do it. I am an American. I am here to bring you to the United States. But we must hurry."

"How do I know you are not KGB? That you are not going to take us out and kill us?" Boris Walensky asked.

"If the KGB wanted to kill you, it would have done so long ago, and it wouldn't have needed to spirit you away to do so," the man in the boat replied. "It just wanted to silence you."

"They could say I was fleeing with an American agent when we were caught and killed in a fight," Boris said.

"Then you will just have to trust me," the man answered. "If I am who I say I am, you will be restored to your honored place in physics. You will be with your colleagues again, not in some wasteland moving stones and garbage. If I am not who I say I am, you and your family will be killed. But you are among the walking dead already."

Boris turned and began to walk back to his hut. Then, he turned. "We will back in a few moments. I hope you have warm clothing for us."

Minutes later, Boris, Rivka, and Gregor were on the small boat, which silently slipped away from the shore. They were soon wrapped in a thick fog. And without wind, the boat moved only with the out-going tide. The man left the till, picked up an oar, and began quietly paddling down the river in the direction of the Laptev Sea.

"Where are we going?" Rivka asked.

The man put a finger to his lips. Then he whispered, "Soon."

Out of the swirl, a small red light blinked. The fog seemed to turn a hard white. Suddenly, the white became a solid wall. The wall turned into a giant white plane whose door was opening wide. Two men in black appeared, one carrying a machine gun. The other put a hook on the front of the boat, drew it close, tied its back and swiftly pulled the Walenskys inside the plane. The beard-ed sailor lowered the sail and collapsed its mast.

"No evidence left behind," he said in his perfect Russian. As the two men in black strapped the boat down, the man ushered his passengers forward. "There are seats up here." As they sat, he fastened safety belts around their waists.

Gregor, who had been too frightened to speak throughout their journey, felt his courage and curiosity returning. "What kind of plane is this? Where are you taking us?" he asked.

"This is called a flying boat. We are taking you to the United States if we can avoid the Soviet radar and fighter planes. As he strapped himself into his seat, he said something in English to the pilots. The plane's engines roared to life. It began coasting down the Lena, slowly at first, then faster and faster. Suddenly they were airborne and rising out of the fog into a starry night and a new life.

15

WHO'S IN CHARGE?

Joey Klugman's first stop of the day was the office of General Horatio Stockton.

He did not have an appointment, but he was sure the general would see him. The sergeant major at the front desk, however, was far less certain. "You don't have an appointment; you don't go in," he said.

Joey regretted that he was in uniform. The sergeant major held a significantly higher status in the military than a master sergeant. But Joey was not playing by the ordinary rules. "With all due respect Sergeant Major, I am with the CID," Joey said, flashing his badge. "Tell the general he can see me here and now or he can see me in Washington while the Army Chief of Staff looks on, and he faces dereliction of duty. And you might very well be in the next room facing similar charges if you don't communicate my message."

The sergeant major was not so much impressed as amused. "The general had you pegged right, feisty fellow," he responded as he pressed the intercom. "Terribly sorry to interrupt, sir. But I have the master sergeant you told me to expect. He insists on seeing you now."

"Send him in as soon as General Dobson leaves," Shorty Stockton replied. "That should take no more than five minutes." Klugman cooled his heels in a chair facing the master sergeant, wishing there was something on his desk to read upside down. The beefy sergeant major looked at Klugman. "The name's Case. If you need anything in here, let me know."

"Thanks," Joey replied. "What's going on, Sergeant Major?" he continued by way of making meaningless conversation.

"You can call me Corky, not Case. My friends call me Corky. I see from the ribbons you did all your fighting in Korea. I was with the general through all of that. He's a good man. A good soldier. You're not here to dirty him, are you?"

"I'm here to investigate the death of a captain. General Stockton has asked me to keep him informed and to look to him for any help. That's it, in a nutshell, Sergeant Major," Joey responded.

"Call me Corky," the beefy man repeated with a smile.

A few moments later, Joey entered Stockton's office.

Shorty Stockton looked as if he'd just come from the barber shop. His hair was neatly cropped, his face shaven to a silky smoothness, his fatigues pressed, his pistol at the ready. They exchanged salutes.

"Well, Klugman, how's the investigation going? And what the hell happened to your face?" the general asked.

"The investigation is going just fine. And you know damn well what happened to my face. A bunch of goons were beating the crap out of me when a squad of cavalry showed up and beat the crap out of them. I was glad to see them, but they were your cavalry, And they shouldn't have been there. Your men were following me, and I want them off my tail. Now!" Joey answered.

Horatio Stockton flushed. "You are forgetting who wears the stars in this room, Sergeant. If I decide to put a tank battalion on your tail, I will put a tank battalion on your tail. I give the orders around here, not some pipsqueak enlisted man with more balls than brains."

Joey did not back down. "If I have to, I will ask the provost general to have you back off. He got his orders from a deputy secretary of defense who also has called in the civilian FBI. In the end, your interference will only slow down this investigation."

Shorty Stockton drew himself up to his full five feet, three and a half inches, puffed out his chest and marched back and forth behind his desk.

Despite being short and tending to fat, Stockton had finished number two in his class at West Point. He had done it with will and intelligence and desire, more desire than his more physically endowed classmates could ever achieve. This need to excel drove him through a spectacular military career. But what truly made him stand out was his theatrics. He had learned from Douglas MacArthur that for leadership to be recognized, it must be spectacular. It must have flair, not simply competence.

"I will make you a deal, Sergeant," he said. "I will withdraw my people and tell you all I know, if you lay all your cards on the table and tell me all you and your FBI friends know."

Joey had read Shorty Stockton's file before leaving Fort Belvoir. He was courageous and daring in combat; his swift Patton-like tank sweeps often catching the enemy off guard leading to impressive victories. Occasionally, he would run his tanks out of fuel, leaving them vulnerable on the battlefield. He was a risk taker. He was ambitious. Yet, he protected his men and was honest with those below as well as above.

"I'll take your deal," Joey replied.

"Good," Stockton said. "Now talk."

"You first, General. I'm the one taking the lumps," Joey answered.

Shorty Stockton rested his hand on his side arm and glared at Joey. "You are a ballsy son-of-a-bitch," he said. He paused then added, "I like it." He motioned Joey to a chair and sat down behind his desk.

"Okay, here's what I know. There's some top-secret stuff coming out of Fort Knox that's been compromised, given over to the Russkies. Now we are upgrading our tanks, improving our armor, firepower, speed, and agility. But the other guys are doing the same thing. We are ahead of them with that stuff, at least I think so. The scuttlebutt is we are going to be getting tactical atomic weapons, something they are nowhere near having.

Now that's the kind of technology they really want to get their hands on. And that's the kind of information that is leaking out of the fort—nuclear stuff. Now, we don't do that kind of experimental work here, except in one place, the rats' nest, the 8-8-5-2. First, I assigned some of my elite troops to serve as security guards over there, so I could have sets of eyes peeking around. They didn't come up with anything."

"That's the real reason I put Manigrove over there, to find out what the hell is going on. He was a shrewd, self-serving bastard, except he was focused more on making a buck than making a career. So, I offered him a buck. I told him that if he came up with the traitor, I would not only promote him to major but would add a year to his retirement. He was pretty close to having his 20 years in, and each year after that would sweeten his pension even more. Anybody else, I would have offered a medal. But he didn't give a damn about medals."

Joey smiled. "And what about my watchdogs?"

"I figured you were a smart, ballsy, loud-mouthed Jew and a patriot to boot. If anybody could ferret out the real bad guy, it would be you. I wanted to know who you were talking with and where you were going. I probably would have let those thugs beat you to a pulp, but Corky Case has a soft spot for war heroes. You can thank him for sending my boys in to save your ass."

"One more thing," Joey said. "Tell me about Sergeant Anthony Villano. Why is he still in the army?"

"Villano is still in the army because he is facing a court martial for burglary and theft from the United States Government. We caught him systematically siphoning off food supplies to our mess halls and burglarizing a post exchange. He should be in a federal prison by now, but his lawyer has won several postponements of his trial, and he has been able to post bail. He's loose because we figured he didn't want to add desertion to his record."

"He fought with me at the Han River," Joey said.

"You mean you saved his ass at the Han River," the general snapped back.

"That's part of it. But he was a good combat soldier. He stood and fought when others ran away," Joey responded.

"You can testify to his soldiering at sentencing," Stockton answered. "Now what have you got for me?"

Joey outlined the case thus far, leaving out details that he thought might jeopardize the investigation. He revealed that Jeffrey Wade was not who he appeared to be. But he did not go beyond that fearing that the case might be tainted if it was revealed the FBI agents had illegally obtained information. He told Stockton that criminals might be using the 8-8-5-2 for some kind of scam, possibly involving Doyle's aide, Lieutenant Carmela Fortunato, and that he might be able to shed some light on that as well as the spying.

The general appeared satisfied. As Joey stood to leave, Shorty Stockton said, "I have a career to protect. I don't intend to let spies or thieves thrive at Fort Knox on my watch. And I don't want announcements involving this fort coming out of the Pentagon. I get to arrest the bad guys first and make some noise first. I know you get my message,

Sergeant. Now be sure to thank the sergeant major on the way out."

"Thanks, Corky," Joey said as he passed the sergeant major's desk.

Corky Case looked up and winked.

16

ELECTRICAL ENGINEERING

Joey had one more stop to make before meeting with the FBI agents. It would be back at the 8-8-5-2, a visit with Corporals Victor Rodney and Frank Marconi, the electrical engineers Manigrove talked to frequently.

After a brief stare at Joey's face and pass, the guard at the gate pointed him toward the electronics laboratory, housed like all the other laboratories in a two-story wooden building painted a dull olive green. As he walked toward the structure, Joey was struck by how much the atmosphere reminded him of a college campus, except that the young men strolling the main quad were dressed in hospital whites, army fatigues, combinations of these uniforms or outfits that bore no resemblance to any military garb. They were chatting and joking. One soldier sat on a bench playing an acoustic guitar and wailing lyrics from Ginsberg's *"Howl."* Four others sat on the grass playing bridge.

He opened the door to the electronics laboratory and asked a technician where he could find Victor Rodney. He was directed to the second floor, the last door on the left.

Joey entered the door to find a dozen men working with devices that sputtered and flashed electric sparks. There were vacuum tubes that pulsated, glowed and dimmed. A generator hummed somewhere. Strips of extremely thin silicone filled two benches. The air smelled of burning ozone.

Moving to a soldier who appeared more occupied with a magazine than electrical equipment, Joey again asked for Rodney. "Who wants to speak to him?" the soldier asked, a wise-assed smile on his face. Joey kicked the chair out from underneath the soldier dumping him on the floor with a loud thud. The noise spun the heads of the engineers, who stared wide-eyed at Joey.

"Holy shit!" a bespectacled young man gasped.

"Now that I have everybody's attention, where is Victor Rodney?"

"You're standing over him!" someone shouted.

Joey looked down in time to see Rodney aiming a fist at his groin. Joey kicked him hard in the ribs, knocking the wind out of him. The kick felt good to Joey. It was nice dishing it out after the beating he had taken. "Now, get nicely to your feet and walk out the door with me, or I'll kick your ass all over your electric wires." With that, he hoisted a groaning Rodney to his feet by the collar of his fatigues. They walked toward the door, and as they left, Joey waved and said, "Carry on, men."

By the time they got to the sunlit street, Rodney had regained most of his wind and all of his arrogance. "I'll get your ass kicked," he yelled at Joey. "I'll get the colonel to kick your ass! Who the hell are you?"

"I'm a detective with the Army's Criminal Investigation Division. And you are facing charges of failing to obey an order, attacking a superior enlisted man and attempting to interfere with an investigation," Joey answered finally letting go of Rodney's collar.

Rodney sought to control himself. He clearly wasn't used to being told what to do. "That's not true," he began. "You knocked me off my chair."

"Tell it to a military judge," Joey snapped back, reaching for a set of handcuffs.

"Put your hands behind your back and don't let me add resisting arrest to the list of charges. Now we are going for a walk."

His hands shackled behind his back, Rodney walked docilely beside Joey toward the gate to the 8-8-5-2. As they passed Doyle's office, Rodney looked plaintively in its direction. Lieutenant Gorgeous looked back in what Joey took for shock. Joey gave her a quick wave and as much of a smile as he could muster from his battered face.

They marched about a quarter mile to a Military Police shack, where Joey introduced himself and requested a few minutes of privacy with the prisoner. "We won't see anything or hear anything, Sarge," one of the MPs said. Then they were gone.

Joey sat Rodney in a hard, wooden chair and stood across from him leaning against a wall. "Now,

Corporal Rodney, I want to ask you a few questions," he began. "You give me honest answers, and I will forget about the charges. You give me dishonest answers, and you will spend time in the stockade. And you know what your fellow prisoners do to weak guys like you. They corn hole them."

Joey paused to let his words sink in. "Okay, question number one. What was your relationship with Captain Albert Ruppert Manigrove III?"

"I knew him, that's all."

"How did you come to know him?"

"He approached me and said he'd heard I was taking book on the horses and sports games. He said he was looking for some action. I told him I didn't do that stuff, but if he wanted some action, I could put him in touch with people who might take it. Hey, I don't want any trouble. I'm not the unit bookie."

"Somehow, if I ask around, I think I could find people who say otherwise," Joey responded. "So, who do you lay off your action with? C'mon Victor. I know you don't have the bread to finance an operation. Your folks cut you off."

"You spoke to my parents?" Rodney asked.

"Not yet. It depends on how cooperative you are," answered Joey. "Again, who do you lay off action with?"

Rodney lowered his head. "I don't take any action, but if I did, I would lay it off with Sergeant Tony Villano. He's a drill sergeant with a basic training company."

Joey felt as if he'd been punched. But he pressed on. "Would you meet with him at *The Twelve Angry Men*?" Joey asked.

His prisoner looked up in surprise. "Yes. You know him?"

"I ask the questions," Joey replied. "Do you do any other business with him?"

Rodney's body went into a bob and weave. "No. No business. I never even said I laid off bets with him."

The corporal was clearly very uncomfortable. There has to be something more here, Joey thought.

"Did he ever talk to you about selling military secrets?" he asked

"Military secrets?" Rodney repeated, seeming to grope for time. "No. Never. We work on some crazy stuff up in the lab. But nobody talked about it. And he didn't ask me about it."

Joey sensed that there was a lot more. "I'll ask you again. Did Captain Manigrove ask you about military secrets?"

"No. We took an oath to keep our mouths shut when we came here. I swear I don't talk about those things." Then he looked up at Joey. "The only thing he talked to me about was making money."

"You don't make money betting the ponies unless you are the bookie," Joey pressed on. "You said you weren't the bookie. Yet you are wearing a top of the line Omega watch. Is there any other way of making money at the 8-8-5-2?"

Rodney again went into his bob and weave. "How would I know? I only work here."

"Now, to walk out of here, all you have to tell me is who killed the captain, why and how?"

Victor Rodney's blue eyes narrowed. A drop of sweat gleamed on his nose then gently splashed onto his fatigue jacket, making a dark, black circle. "I don't know anything about that," he said.

"That's a dishonest answer. It puts you a step closer to the stockade."

"All I know is that he ran up a big betting tab. I swear that's all I know."

"Maybe that's an honest answer, maybe not," Joey responded. "I'll get back to you on that one."

He walked behind Rodney's chair and flipped out its back legs.

Victor Rodney fell to his knees and rolled over to avoid hitting his head. Joey bent over him. "Answer this, and I'll let you go," Joey said. "Was Manigrove looking for a piece of the action?"

"You'd have to ask Sergeant Villano. I don't know," Rodney screeched.

"I think you do," said Joey. He rolled the chair over forcing Rodney's head to bang off the floor. He opened the handcuffs. "Get out of here," he said.

Rodney stumbled to his feet and ran out the door.

17

HI-FI'S AND TV'S

Joey returned to General Stockton's office; Sergeant Major "Corky" Case greeted him like an old comrade in arms. "Hear you been kickin' ass and takin' names," he said, nostalgia for such things clinging to his tone.

"Don't believe everything you hear Sergeant Major," Joey replied. "Just some routine questioning."

Still, the speed of the report from the MPs to the garrison commander surprised Joey. "You folks still following me around?" he asked.

"I'm beginning to like you more and more, young fellow," Case responded, clearly choosing not to respond to the question. "And just call me Corky," he added.

Joey smiled. "I'll do that, Sergeant Major," he said. "By the way, I was wondering whether there were any messages for me?"

"Indeed, indeed," Case replied. "Your FBI friends stopped by and said to tell you Laurens had some business in Elizabethtown and Conrad will meet you at the motel. They said to tell you to dress up for supper at the *Old House Restaurant* at 432 South Fifth Street in Louisville, 1900 hours. That's a nice place for genuine Southern food. You'll enjoy it."

"Will one of your boys be waiting tables?" Joey asked.

"You are a suspicious, young fellow, aren't you?" Case shot back, again not answering the question. "Oh, you had one other message, from a Mike Theiss. He declined to identify himself any further. Said you should call him. You are welcome to use the phone on my desk."

"I wouldn't dream of it," Joey responded. "I know you are disappointed, but the call can wait."

"As you wish," Case answered with a sigh that suggested trust. "Mind sharing with me the identity of this Theiss gentleman?"

"As a matter of fact, yes," answered Joey and left.

With his tough guy reputation, now preceding him, Joey decided to return to the electronics laboratory and speak to Corporal Frank Marconi before he disappeared or matched his story to Rodney's. When he entered the laboratory this time, all work stopped. A first lieutenant had joined the enlisted men and asked Joey what he wanted. "The work being done here is secret, Sergeant. You should not be here."

"I have full secret clearance and have been given full access to this facility by Lieutenant Colonel Doyle," Joey answered. "I'm with the CID, and I'm sure you don't want to be accused of impeding an investigation."

"Of course not, but I'm calling the lieutenant colonel to confirm your clearance. And please don't talk to anyone until I return. I'm sure you understand," the officer replied.

"Perfectly," Joey answered.

He saw Victor Rodney hunkered down in a corner, furtively looking in his direction, not knowing what to expect. Joey pulled a roster from his Ike jacket. "I want to see the following men: Pfc. John St. Pierre, Pfc. Bruce Spitzer, and Corporal Frank Marconi. I expect to interview every member of this laboratory," he continued. "And I expect you to be truthful with me."

At that moment, the first lieutenant returned and announced, "We will give full cooperation to Master Sergeant Klugman, who is investigating the death of Captain Manigrove."

Joey would have preferred to keep the point of the investigation vague. But perhaps it was just as well the men related it to Manigrove's death.

Though his decision to question St. Pierre and Spitzer was a spur of the moment device to create a blind for the questioning of Marconi, he decided it would be a good idea to question all of the men in the lab. Somehow, he felt something was going on here that he could not yet put his finger on.

Each man was interviewed separately on the steps of the building housing the electronics unit. St. Pierre and Spitzer said they were working on projects involving the uses of radar and sonar for identifying objects at substantial distances and identifying nearby objects that were close but hidden. As an example, St. Pierre said the Chinese had come up with a particularly crippling wooden landmine known as the "Bouncing Betty." When an infantryman tripped it, the device would jump up about two feet before exploding filling its victim with hundreds of splinters in and around his groin, stomach, and legs. The mine was designed to injure, not to kill, thus removing from combat not only the wounded man but those who came to aid him.

The laboratory's job was to create a "Bouncing Betty" detector that could distinguish this wooden explosive device from a rotting tree limb or piece of timber. "We think we're coming close," St. Pierre said. "It has to do with the properties of the explosive, not the wood."

"What else goes on at the lab?" Joey asked each man.

Both hesitated then replied: "Experimentation, that's all."

"You must be very enthusiastic about your work," Joey pressed. "I hear the lights are on late into the night at the electronics lab."

St. Pierre and Spitzer allowed that they and their co-workers were very enthusiastic about their projects. That bothered Joey. As wacky as this outfit was, it still was made up of soldiers, most of whom were reluctant draftees. They were not giving away free overtime. Somehow, they were making money.

Frank Marconi's interview went very differently. Despite being short, slightly overweight and bespectacled, Marconi gave off a sense of unbounded energy. "It's about time you guys showed up," he said as soon as he and Joey were alone. "There is weird stuff going on here."

"Spies? Traitors?" asked Joey.

"No, crooks. I know about crooks. There may be more going on. But I'm a little out of the loop."

"Crooks?"

"Crooks!" Marconi repeated impatiently. "I told this to that Captain Manigrove.

He didn't do anything, and then he got killed. It's weird I tell you."

"Okay, start at the top. What are the crooks doing?"

"They are making high fidelity radios and televisions and selling them in Louisville."

"That's very entrepreneurial, so what's the crime?" asked Joey.

"You still don't get it," Marconi responded. "They order all their parts through the government, the amplifiers, the pre-amps, the woofers, the tweeters, the vacuum tubes, even those new transistors, everything. The purchase orders are never questioned because our work is secret. We can order anything."

Joey began to understand. "The government supplies the equipment, the laboratory for assembly and the manpower through the draftees. There is no overhead."

"Right," Marconi answered.

"Who runs the operation?"

"Victor Rodney, the guy you beat up. But he works with other people outside our lab."

"Is everyone up there involved?"

"It's strictly voluntary. Maybe half. They work a night shift putting out the commercial product. During the day, the work is high-end secret stuff, no commercial value."

"Everybody is invited in. If you say no, that's okay, just keep your mouth shut. And everybody does. It's kind of a joke. The government screwed you by drafting you. Now you're screwing the government by going into business or keeping your mouth shut."

"Why are you talking?"

Marconi shuffled his feet and blushed. "This may sound stupid to you. But I think stealing is wrong, and I believe you don't turn your back on crimes. That's the way I was brought up. My family worked hard to get me an engineering degree. In fact, I'm the first in my family to go to college. But I was told you get what you want through hard work and a day's work for a day's pay, in other words, honesty."

"I don't think you're stupid at all," Joey replied. "But I have to know more. How and when do they ship the hi-fi's and televisions out of here? Where do the trucks come from? Who are they delivered to?"

Frank Marconi shrugged his shoulders. "I don't know. I'm not in on the deal. And they don't like me. I think they know I went to Manigrove. I don't know what they might do if they found out I talked to you. But I'll try to get you some more answers."

"Do you know why the captain was killed?"

Again, Marconi shrugged. "Maybe he was gathering evidence, and they caught him."

"Would you be willing to testify to everything you know?" Joey asked.

"Sure," Marconi replied without a shrug or hesitation.

"I'll get back to you," Joey answered.

Marconi smiled. He turned and walked back into the building.

18

GIG BUSINESS

When Joey returned to his motel room, the phone was ringing. It was State Police Detective Mike Theiss. "Where you been? I've been trying to catch up with you all day!" he shouted.

"Not so loud," Joey responded. "I already got ear damage from all the shelling I had to listen to. Now, what have you got?"

"I did some research on whether any kind of contraband was moving from Knox to Louisville. The word on the street is a bunch of petty stuff is being stolen out of the PXs—cigarettes, shaving gear, shirts, magazines, anything that makes a quick sale.

There's also been meat disappearing from shipments to the fort and showing up in Louisville's butcher shops. But you'll never guess the biggest traffic, doing $5,000 a week," Theiss said, sounding particularly smug.

"Hi-fi sets and televisions," Joey broke in.

"Damn, you knew!" Theiss shouted frustrated that his surprise was no surprise.

"I just found out. I've got a guy willing to talk, but he only knows about the assembly end of it. He's a blank on how the completed equipment is picked up and sold," Joey answered.

Joey then gave the detective a run down on his conversations with Frank Marconi and Victor Rodney. "I intend to question all of them in the electronics lab," Joey added. "I'm sure I'll get others to talk, once they realize I know."

"Good. I'll keep the pressure on the locals to find out how the distribution system works. The word on the street says that the organized crime boys are involved and that the sets are not only sold in Louisville but all along the East Coast." Theiss hung up wondering whether he was dealing with the biggest case of his career.

Joey had stripped off his Class A uniform and was about to take a shower when a knock came at the motel door. He had just taken off his ankle holster. He quietly removed the .32 caliber pistol, held it lightly in his hand and stepped to the side of the door. "Yes?" he said.

"It's me, Anita."

"Hold a second. I've got to put on some pants," Joey answered, slipping back into his uniform trousers.

He opened the door, holding the .32 in his free hand. Anita Conrad stepped in and gasped. "I'll put down the gun," Joey said.

"It's not the gun. It's those welts and bruises on your back and chest. Some of them broke the scar tissue on old bullet wounds. You may have some broken ribs. You should have gone to a hospital" she said.

"I don't have time for a hospital right now. Besides, I'm feeling better," Joey replied.

"I'm a doctor, let me check you out," Anita said. She didn't wait for a reply. She simply ran her hands gently along his bruises. Joey winced. Even her light, warm touch made him ache.

"You should get x-rayed," she concluded.

"Okay, but not today, too much to do," Joey said.

She had completed her examination and was now looking up into his eyes. Then she moved a finger softly along his lips. "Tough kid from the city," she said smiling. "Us girls from Long Island always found city boys enticing but dangerous, like forbidden candy. Maybe too rough, maybe not enough respect." She was looking up at him with those sparkling dark gray eyes. Joey bent his head slightly and kissed her softly on the lips. He felt her mouth open, and he moved his tongue inside. They clung together for a long moment. Then she pulled away.

"Not now, maybe later," she said gasping for air.

"I thought you were involved with Laurens," Joey managed.

"Strictly professional," Anita answered. "I think he would like to make it more.

"He's good looking enough. But he's too cold, too Jimmy Stewart for a girl from Rockville Centre. I like warmth, passion. I'm part Italian, you know."

"What's the other part?" Joey asked.

"Later," she responded. "I didn't come to your room for lovemaking."

"Then what?"

"First to check you out medically and second to update you on my research.

Medically, all things considered, you are fine. Maybe more than fine. You seemed able to handle my lips quite well," she answered.

"That was a medical test?" Joey asked.

"Medicine is an art form," Anita answered. "A lot goes into a diagnosis, which relates to some of what I found. The 8-8-5-2 is deeply involved in a lot of cutting-edge medical experimentation, for example lowering body temperature in preparation for surgery. They, of course, are doing advanced work in radioactivity. And they also are doing something that requires large quantities of wafer thin slivers of silicon and another mineral called germanium. No one at the Defense Department or the Surgeon General's Office knows what it is for. It is not on their assigned task list. But the brass has been hesitant to question the mineral purchases since government policy is to let science do its thing without interference. But there is something very fishy about all this."

"I saw the silicon today in the electronics lab," Joey said. "It was laid out in very thin strips."

Anita sat quietly on Joey's bed for a moment. "Have you heard of the Nike and Titan missiles?" she asked.

"Vaguely, technologically enhanced artillery," Joey responded.

"Something like that. They require very complicated, very accurate and very small guidance and control systems to put them on target. Some scientists are working with germanium and silicon to miniaturize and integrate these systems. The Defense Department has financed micromodule or molecular electronic systems, without much success. But it has not invested in the mineral approach."

"Which brings us back to what is silicon doing in the 8-8-5-2's electronic lab," Joey said.

Anita looked at her watch and rose suddenly. "We must be on our way shortly. I'll leave you to dress. We can drive to the restaurant together," she said and left.

After he showered and changed into civilian clothes, Joey pondered another question, the one he was supposed to answer: How did Captain Albert Ruppert Manigrove III fit into all of this? If Marconi was to be believed, the captain was aware of the traffic in electronic equipment between the 8-8-5-2 and the city. Then why didn't he act? Why didn't he arrest anybody? Maybe he was trying to put together the entire network before coming down on its members. They could have realized what he was doing and killed him. Or he could have joined their scheme. If his career said anything, it was that he was motivated by money.

Then again, General Stockton had put him in the unit to find out if someone was leaking secret information to the Soviets. Nothing thus far indicated that Manigrove had found out anything about spying— unless he had found some connection between the crooks and the spies. But what?

Joey wore a loose and colorful Hawaiian shirt over tan chinos for his supper with the federal agents. While he did not favor wearing shirts that overlapped his trim waistline, they did have the advantage of concealing his .38 caliber service revolver. He also continued to wear his ankle holster with its snug little .32 tucked inside. He still owed somebody for the beating he had taken the other night.

19

SAVING THE WORLD

The *Old House Restaurant* lived up to its reputation. It had the warm, friendly ambiance of a well-lived-in home, all wood and silver. Off, in a corner table far away from the main part of the restaurant sat Mark Laurens. His light blue eyes seemed focused somewhere inside the tiny flame that topped the candle on his table. And his large hands opened and closed around the drink in front of him. Joey sensed physical power in the man restrained only by an act of will. Laurens could be a very tough, nasty guy.

"Sorry we're late," Anita said as she and Joey sat down.

Laurens looked up with a hard smile. "I know Klugman's routine. Always a little late, a little sorry, maybe. But I didn't know it was catching," he said.

Anita blushed but said nothing.

Glancing at Klugman, Laurens said, "That's a wild kind of shirt, man. Planning on doing a hula? Trouble is it makes you stand out in a crowd."

Joey sensed he was being reprimanded, but he didn't know why. Something was up, and he had not been clued in.

"You didn't tell him?" Laurens asked Anita

"No, I thought we should tell him together," she answered

"So, you let him come as a barber pole," her partner snapped. "So, anyone who knew him or had a picture of him would know he is here—badge, gun, and handcuffs."

"Hey," Joey cut in. "I pick my own clothes. Nobody paid particular attention when I walked in. I look like some Yankee tourist, that's all."

"Okay," answered Laurens, not wishing a confrontation with Joey. "Apparently, no damage."

Then he turned his head slightly in the direction of the main part of the restaurant. "There's a chunky man in his mid-50s sitting at a table almost directly ahead of us," he continued. "He is Vladimir Karpov, a colonel in the Soviet KGB. He is Wade's contact. We have agents at surrounding tables as well as outside."

"Talk about being out of the loop," Joey said. "This is crap. I'm supposed to be heading this assignment. And you set this up without a word to me."

"No way to reach you. I thought Anita would update you," Laurens shot back.

Joey shot Anita a hard look. She mumbled another weak, "Sorry."

"So, you confirmed Wade is passing information to this Karpov," Joey said.

"Well, not exactly," Laurens replied. "We put wiretaps on all the public pay phones near the 8-8-5-2 as soon as we got here, figuring whoever is spying is too smart to use an army phone to talk to his contact. Soon after we interviewed Wade, he went to one of those phones and called an Igor Nabicov at a motel not far from where we are staying. He spoke to this Nabicov in Russian. We had the tape rushed to Washington, where their conversation was translated. Wade said: 'I have become too busy to play chess with you this evening.' Nabicov responded: 'I completely understand' and hung up. We immediately put a surveillance team on him. They got a picture of him, and our people identified him as Colonel Vladimir Karpov of the KGB. They were a little surprised that a ranking type like Karpov would be acting as a spy handler. This Wade must be giving away dynamite."

"Yes," responded Joey. "But if this guy has been warned, why is he hanging around a Louisville restaurant? Why didn't he make for the train station or the airport or the bus terminal?"

"All we know," said Anita, "is that a second call came in and a clear American voice told Karpov: '7:30, *Old House Restaurant*' and hung up."

The dining room had begun to fill up, and it was hard keeping an eye on the Russian without becoming obvious. Two elderly women with extremely large hats had been seated between the agents and their target. They soon were joined by two large men, who already were enjoying golden bourbon from deep, ice-filled tumblers. They had diverted to the bar while their wives were being escorted to their seats.

A waiter approached the agents' table. For the first time, Joey looked at the menu. It offered a variety of Southern dishes as well as classic French fare. "If you've never had it, I would suggest getting some home cooking," said Laurens in his deep down South accent. "A bowl of she-crab soup for an appetizer, then Southern fried chicken with grits and collard greens would be a wonderful supper."

"I think for now I'll have a Jack Daniels on the rocks with a twist of lemon," Joey told the waiter.

"Make that two," said Laurens.

"Just a coke for me, and give us a few more minutes before the food order," Anita added.

The waiter nodded, politely and went off for the drinks. "Surveillance takes my appetite away," Joey said.

"A shame," Laurens responded.

Joey began to appreciate the agent's dry wit.

Just then a tall, thin figure entered the dining room. Though he was wearing civilian clothes now, there was no mistaking Lieutenant Colonel Francis X. Doyle, the skull-like face, the thinning, straw-colored hair. He moved directly to Karpov's table and sat down.

"God bless!" Laurens gasped.

"Holy shit!" said Joey almost simultaneously.

"Our traitor!" Anita declared.

"Let's pick them up," whispered Laurens.

"Not yet," said Joey. "Let's see just how friendly they are. We can arrest them when they leave."

"I wish I'd bugged their table," Laurens muttered.

The gregarious Karpov stood up and reached a beefy hand toward Doyle. Doyle grasped it with bony fingers. "The good Colonel Doyle," Karpov said. "What was so urgent that I should delay fleeing to speak to you?"

"We have been useful to each other," Doyle answered.

"Agreed, and since I must endanger myself in respect for you, I have decided to have one last Southern meal while we talk. Please, order something," Karpov said pointing toward a menu. "I shall have the barbecue ribs."

"Just sweet tea for me," Doyle responded.

"So why are we here?" Karpov asked.

"As you Soviets undoubtedly know, in March, the United States set off an actual hydrogen bomb, not just a device, at Bikini Atoll in the Marshall Islands. It was light enough to be dropped from a plane. The explosion was far more powerful than scientists had predicted. It was equivalent to a thousand atomic bombs going off at once. It also spewed an unexpectedly massive amount of radiation. The outside world does not know this yet, but Japanese fishermen 90 miles away from the epicenter were poisoned by this radiation and likely will die. There is no cure for this kind of human damage. A hydrogen bomb exchange would end the human race and every other living thing except perhaps for cockroaches. You Russians must understand this. This super bomb is not a military option. It is the destroyer of the world."

"Yes, we understand all too well," Karpov answered. "It is you Americans who do not understand. You go forward again and again with ever larger weapons of mass destruction. When you stop, we will stop."

"All I can hope is that a balance of terror will prevail between the superpowers. I have here in an envelope details on the findings from the hydrogen bomb tests. Your scientists will understand. And they must convey their understanding to the Communist leadership. That is essential if we humans are to survive," answered Doyle.

Karpov slipped the envelope inside his jacket and began to devour a shrimp cocktail appetizer.

"I have a second reason for meeting with you directly," Doyle said. "I want you to save Jeffrey Wade. The FBI is on to his real identity. And it is only a matter of time before they link him to you. I want you to get him out. Return him to Russia, where he will be a tremendous asset to your scientific community."

"Ah, the passionate Gregor. Yes, I am sure he would be a welcome addition to our scientists. I understand he is almost as good as his father and less than half his age. We could expect much from him. Except, I would very much fear he would turn our secrets over to the CIA. You see, he is a humanitarian, like yourself, not a patriot."

"Here, he will go to jail," said Doyle

"He probably would go to jail in my country, and your jails are much nicer places I am given to understand," answered the KGB man. "So, given a choice . . . " Karpov let the rest of his sentence hang.

Doyle pondered for a moment. "What if I can give you his father as well? Then you would have both, each insurance for the loyalty of the other."

"I thought you did not know where Walensky is?"

"I don't, but I think Jeffrey will tell me—and I have other sources. After all, there are very few premiere nuclear physicists in this country, and they tend to be in contact with each other."

Karpov welcomed the waiter carrying his barbecue ribs and dug in with an enthusiastic appetite. After a moment, he wiped his hands on an enormous white napkin and said, "You have a deal. I will spirit Gregor out of the United States if you locate Boris Walensky for me. But we have little time. As careful as we have been, we assuredly have left a trail. So, you finish your tea. I will forgo dessert. I have a taxi waiting and a train to catch."

"And the Walenskys will work for you as scientists. They will not be imprisoned," Doyle said anxiously.

"Of course," the KGB man answered. "We are practical people. As long as we have each of them as insurance for the other, they will be, if not loyal, at least faithful to us."

They rose. Karpov paid the bill and left a generous tip. "We Communists must always think of the workers," he said with a chuckle. "Besides, I have an expense account. Perhaps I am a capitalist after all."

The tall, skeletal Doyle and the beefy Karpov exited the restaurant into what had become a cool night. "Your Kentucky fall sometimes carries a chill," the Russian said.

20

ARREST AND DETENTION

"**You** are under arrest." The voice came from somewhere back of them out of the dark shadows of the parking lot.

Karpov and Doyle spun around simultaneously. Though the overhead light had turned the figure into a shadow, Doyle instantly recognized the voice. "Klugman!" he gasped.

"And the FBI," said Laurens from somewhere out in front of them. "Please, don't resist."

Doyle had long known this moment would come. He thought he had prepared for it. He would express a sense of outrage, then denial, then demand a lawyer. But now that it was real, he could do none of those things. For the moment, all he felt was shock, a weakness in his legs, and unexpectedly, fear. Karpov was more professional. "This must be some kind of mistake. I am a businessman," he said, expressing the outrage Doyle could not find. My name is Igor Nabokov. You can look at my passport."

"You are a goddamn spy!" Laurens shot back. "Now put your hands behind you. You are about to be handcuffed." Both men submitted passively. Each was patted down. Neither was armed. When Laurens reached inside Karpov's jacket and pulled out a thick envelope, the KGB man protested. "You have no right to examine my private papers," he said. "I know my rights in this country. This is unconstitutional search and seizure."

"Bullshit," answered Klugman.

The envelope was passed to Anita, who glanced at its contents quickly. "It's everything on the hydrogen bomb," she said. "Data and conclusions."

The pair was pushed into an unmarked FBI van and driven to the bureau's local headquarters. It was a gray, two-story building that had once been a bank. Its doors and walls were thick and gray. Two large pictures faced all those entering. One was of a grinning President Dwight Eisenhower. The other was of a dour J. Edgar Hoover. The lighting gave Hoover's glare a dominance that reduced Ike's grin to a weak smile, hinting at the real power in Washington.

They were separated for interrogation. The agents would question Karpov. Joey would question Doyle. The interrogation rooms were bare, with green walls and gray ceilings. Each room contained several chairs placed around a wooden table. On top of each table sat a bulky black tape recorder. Large fluorescent lights sprayed a pasty white glow over the interrogators and their subjects.

Both men were shown photos of Doyle handing Karpov the envelope containing the secret information.

"Mostly, I see a picture of two ladies' big hats," Karpov said. They sparred for a time over exactly what the photograph showed. Karpov maintained for a time that he truly was Igor Nabokov. Yes, he was a Russian by birth, but he had long ago become a Czechoslovakian citizen and carried that country's passport. He was in the import-export business and was trying to sell Czech linens in the United States. He was introduced to Doyle by Jeffrey Wade, whom he had met at a local chess tournament. "You have no idea how boring it can be, living in a strange city knowing no one. And I have become too old and fat to chase women. So I watch and play chess," Karpov told them. He had no idea what was in the envelope Doyle had given him. "All I know is that he asked me to hold on to it for a while. And that he would ask for it back."

At this point, Laurens pulled out the FBI's file on Colonel Vladimir Karpov. "This is you," said Laurens showing him a long lens photograph of a somewhat younger Karpov in uniform walking toward Lubyanka Prison.

"Ah, but much thinner, a charming picture," Karpov said. "Yes, no need to play games any longer. I am Colonel Vladimir Karpov. I .am an attaché at the Soviet embassy in Washington, D.C., and I have diplomatic immunity."

Laurens walked behind the hard chair on which Karpov was seated and in one swift motion yanked him to his feet. Hardly had the KGB man stood up, then Laurens smashed his fist into his captive's kidney. Karpov expelled a mixture of air and scream and fell back into the chair.

"So much for your immunity, you spying son-of-a-bitch," Laurens hissed. 'Now I want you to tell me two things. First, why did you kill Captain Manigrove? Second, how much secret information did you get from Comrade Gregor Walensky?"

Karpov turned toward Laurens with a look of surprise. "I had nothing to do with your Captain Manigrove, alive or dead."

Laurens struck Karpov hard just above his ear. The blow knocked him off his chair and onto the hard, concrete floor. A trickle of blood began to flow from Karpov's nose. He stared up at Laurens. "I tell you again; I know nothing of the captain's death." Laurens pointed shoe slammed into Karpov's ribs. Karpov groaned and vomited.

"Stop," Anita said her voice sharp and commanding. "We don't have to go through this, Colonel. I believe you are telling the truth."

The FBI man looked at his colleague. "How the hell do you know?" he asked, his face now a hard mask.

"I've been through interrogations before," she answered.

"So have I," Laurens replied, yanking Karpov back onto his chair. "Now, I'm going to get some answers."

"Not that way," Anita responded. "Touch him one more time, and I'll have you up on charges."

Laurens looked as if he would strike Anita. Then, after a long moment, he softened. "Okay, okay," he said. "You talk to him."

Anita moved closer to Karpov. "I'm sorry my associate got carried away. But we do need your cooperation. Just give us something, anything, so we can tell our superiors you cooperated." She removed his handcuffs.

Karpov took out a handkerchief and wiped the blood away from his nose. "I appreciate your efforts. As someone who has had the responsibility of extracting information from reluctant individuals, I understand the necessity to create stress and to offer the opportunity to relieve that stress. But I can tell you only that I had heard about this Captain Manigrove and nothing more."

"What had you heard?" Anita pressed.

"That he was asking questions about unauthorized activities at the 8-8-5-2," Karpov responded.

"You mean spying?" the woman agent asked.

"Perhaps. I don't know. I never met him."

"Who told you about him?"

"Colonel Doyle, I believe." Karpov dabbed again at his nose.

"What did he say?"

"That this strange captain was asking a lot of questions about things that had nothing to do with discipline. He thought he was some kind of covert agent."

"For whom?"

"He didn't know. He suspected the fort's commanding general."

"Now tell us about your relationship with Jeffrey Wade."

"There is not much to tell. He and I met at a chess club. I immediately recognized his accent as Russian, and we began to converse in our native tongue. We both enjoy the game, and occasionally we would meet to play."

"He never told you his Russian name?"

"He did say that I could call him Gregor, but that was all. He never talked about his departure from the Soviet Union or his family."

"You expect us to believe that?"

"Believe what you like," Karpov answered, instinctively twisting away from an expected blow from Laurens. It did not come. But Laurens moved closer.

"Did Gregor give you secret information?" Anita asked gently.

"No," the Soviet colonel said quickly.

Laurens grabbed Karpov's collar. Just then a knock came, and a crew-cut man entered. "Got to speak to you," he said to the agents. "Out here."

Laurens swiftly handcuffed Karpov's hands to the back of the chair. "I have no intention of committing suicide," the KGB man said.

"And you won't, unless you are a contortionist," Laurens responded and left.

"We just got a call from State," the crew-cut man said. "The Soviet Embassy is demanding to know where one of their attaches is, a man named Igor Nabokov. The Russkies believe we have him and are in a real tizzy. Washington says we should move him to our D.C. facility and that he should look in good shape. We have a plane waiting."

"We'll clean him up," Laurens replied.

He and Anita returned to the interrogation room. Laurens removed the handcuffs.

"Colonel, we have just been ordered to have you transported to our Washington office," Anita said. "We have no idea how you will be treated there, but it could be very difficult for you. They have special interrogators with authorization to do whatever they wish. We can't protect you there. But if you tell us all you know about Gregor, we will be able to keep you here under our care."

Karpov smiled. "I appreciate your concern for my welfare, but I have nothing further to tell you or your interrogators in Washington. Let them do what they wish," he answered and gingerly stood up. "I am sure my embassy has been looking for me since I did not call in at the required hour. And I am sure they have contacted your State Department."

Laurens handed him a wet towel and said, "Wipe your face."

"You would feel right at home in my organization, young man," Karpov replied. "And I have learned something about how you play bad cop, good cop in this country from your lovely associate." He smiled at Anita. "Dasvidanya," he added as the crew-cut man led him away.

21

DOYLE'S REVENGE

Joey Klugman turned his chair backward, straddled it and grasped the back with both hands. Doyle sat straight in a chair across the table that separated them. He stared at his captor with the look of a cornered lion—no fear, no retreat, no regrets, just the sense that he would die gallantly.

Joey stared back, trying to cross a divide wider than the Mississippi to understand what this man had done. Why would a third-generation American, a member of this country's natural aristocracy, its intellectual elite, betray all that it had given to him? Why would he endanger a place so cherished by Joey's parents?

Joey felt no hatred, not even anger toward this man, only a sad incomprehension.

"Why?" he finally asked.

Doyle put aside his long-prepared plan. There would be no outrage, no denial, no demand for an attorney. This would be his opportunity to lay his case before the world in some open court. Conviction for treason, perhaps the death penalty, would make his case even stronger. He would become a martyr. The moment of weakness and shame was gone. He would defend what he had done both as retribution for what America had done to him and others as a justifiable, humanitarian act to save the world.

"Why?" he retorted. "Are you capable of grasping why?"

"Colonel, I nearly died for my country. It ordered me to fight, and I fought. I did it without a second's thought. America gave my parents a refuge and me the opportunity to live my life as I saw fit. Yes, I would have trouble grasping why you betrayed this wonderful place. I suspect you believed you had good reasons to do so. But I'm not here to judge you. That's for some court. I'm here to gather the facts."

For the first time in a long time, Doyle smiled. "I never took you for a fool. I knew they wouldn't send a fool after me twice. One Manigrove was enough. But I must admit, I expected my hunter to be, well, more like myself. Instead, I was confronted with what I thought was merely a bright policeman, someone who chooses not to distinguish between good and evil, traitor or humanitarian, the thief who steals a loaf of bread or the one who robs a bank. On that premise, I thought I could throw you off by having you beaten, by having you believe you were dealing with crude mobsters. My mistake. I now see that the policeman is also a patriot."

"You ordered my beating? Through whom?" Joey asked.

"That thug, Villano," Doyle answered.

"I don't believe you," Joey shot back.

"Believe what you will," Doyle answered

"What information did you give to the Soviets and why?" asked Joey, shifting to the main purpose of the interrogation.

As the tape whirred, Doyle drew Joey back into a world he was only vaguely aware of. It was early 1943; a young Frances X. Doyle had just earned his Ph.D. at New England University in nuclear physics. He also had acquired a beautiful wife named Kathleen. She had recently received her medical degree and was specializing in the effects of radiation on health. Their work dovetailed as beautifully as their lives. Together, they explored the very nature of things.

World War II, however, was about to intervene. Armies were on the march everywhere, and Doyle knew that he would soon be drafted. Then Stafford Warren, a highly-respected radiologist at the university, took him into his office, closed the door and changed his life. He asked Doyle to join a top secret national effort to create an atomic bomb. It was called The Manhattan Project. Laboratories were set up in Oak Ridge Tennessee, Los Alamos, New Mexico and elsewhere.

Doyle hesitated. He was astonished that anyone would want to build such a weapon. "Such a bomb could kill thousands," he said.

"We know. But the Germans are already working on it, and even Einstein has urged its development here," said Warren. "If we don't get it first, the Nazis could rule the world for the next thousand years."

Doyle agreed to join the Manhattan Project, then joined the military as a captain in the United States Army. Kathleen joined him as a civilian member of the team. While Francis toiled at solving the technological problems of splitting the atom, Kathleen worked at potential results. Scientists then knew little about the radioactive effects of the bomb's components—uranium, plutonium, and polonium—on human beings. But they had their suspicions. The fate of the workers who painted glow-in-the-dark radium on the faces of watches was well known.

Perhaps the explosion of an atom bomb would not only release tremendous energy but spray silent killer rays for miles. They would offer no telltale smell or taste or feel to their victims. They would simply enter their bodies and destroy them from the inside.

Kathleen and her fellow health professionals gathered data from the fluids and physical examinations of the hundreds of workers employed by the Manhattan Project. Many were knowingly or unknowingly in contact with radioactive materials on a daily basis. Experiments also were being conducted on animals. But the results were still insufficient for the project's managers. The unanswered question was what effect an atomic blast would have on human beings?

In 1944, researchers began injecting radioactive materials into unsuspecting patients. Others were subjected to external radiation. The problem was that people who were already sick might react differently from healthy individuals. Some within the research group decided to experiment on their healthy colleagues—with or without their knowledge. Kathleen was one of their victims. She died a slow, agonizing death.

"I recognized her symptoms. And I soon learned she had been deliberately exposed. But, we had no cure. I had to sit and watch helplessly as this beautiful, wonderful woman died before my eyes. I never forgave the military or the government for allowing this to happen. I determined to get my revenge but in a way that would prevent others from suffering her fate. I would stay in the army and share our terrible findings with our deadliest enemy, the Soviet Union. By making the Russians aware of the horrible destructiveness of nuclear weapons, they would understand that there could be no winner in an atomic war. I had several contacts with Soviet agents over the years, but being posted here to head the 8-8-5-2 offered me what seemed my best cover. The unit was part of the government's Project Sunshine, a loose confederation of fallout research programs. I, therefore, had access not only to work being done here but throughout the country."

Doyle leaned back in his chair. He felt a sense of relief in telling Joey, and all he represented, why he had revealed the nation's secrets. Keeping his bitterness buried for so long had entrapped his own humanity. He had turned inward after the death of his wife. No one had been allowed within his emotional wall until Jeffrey Ward arrived—the youth who could have been his son. He had suppressed too much for too long.

"Did Jeffrey Wade assist you in delivering secrets to the Soviets?" Joey asked.

"No," Doyle replied. "He was a lucky find, that's all. His innocent connection with Igor gave me some cover. I could always say Jeffrey introduced us, that we had a common interest in chess."

"What was your relationship with Carmela Fortunato?" Joey asked.

Doyle let out a soft sigh. "Ah, the lovely seductress. I needed someone who could help me control all these bright, young, arrogant men. What better way than through their sexuality. I let it be known at personnel, informally, that I needed a woman who was bright, a college graduate, pretty and single. The fools immediately thought it was for me."

"Wasn't it?" asked Joey.

Doyle sighed again. "If only that were true. In any event, they produced Carmela. And Carmela, knowing well how to control men, quickly tried to seduce me. She has an instinct for power and willingly uses her sexuality to get that power. I must admit I appreciated her efforts at seduction, but the same radiation that killed my wife robbed me of my libido. In fact, it is slowly robbing me of my life. I was not always the gaunt skeleton you see before you. But day by day, hour by hour, I grow weaker. There is no cure. The end is inevitable."

Joey realized this man had nothing to lose. He would make his last attack upon the government in a United States court of law. It would be his public forum for the exposure of the military's secret practice of human experimentation. He would put the United States government on trial for crimes against humanity.

Joey's sympathy for Doyle rose, but he fundamentally believed that the only thing Doyle's treason had accomplished was to expose the United States' vulnerability to its deadliest enemy. His Korean experience had left him with the sense that the Communists were indifferent to the loss of life in pursuit of their goals. Their soldiers had been used up as so much cannon fodder as they charged into the superior American firepower.

"Carmela quickly recognized my situation and changed her tactics," Doyle continued, "She quickly moved to make life as comfortable as possible in other ways. When my constant pain flared, she would hold me tight in her arms, pressing hard, rocking with me, trying to absorb some of that pain into her own body. It has been as pure a relationship of platonic love as I could have known, or hoped for, though I will never know her sincerity." Tears formed in Doyle's eyes. He wiped them away with a handkerchief and went on.

"She kept my men in check, perhaps doing sexual favors for some of them. I did not inquire. She asked only that she be allowed to operate a discrete private business from within the compound and that she would be using some of our electronics people for her work."

"And you agreed," Joey said.

"Yes. But do not take me for a love-sick fool. I was soon aware that whatever was going on was of questionable legality. I was signing off for purchases of large amounts of electronic gear. I am not an expert in that field, but I knew enough to realize that the jump in these purchases was not warranted from past experience. I also saw this behavior as an opportunity to cover my own activities. General Stockton was nosing around. He suspected me of something. Eventually, he sent that fool Manigrove in. Then you and your FBI friends came along. I told her about my idea of having you roughed up. She knew that would have you chasing after her operation, not traitors. But she was not overly concerned. She said that might be a benefit to her as well. I didn't understand then, and I don't now, but she told me to expect a call from Sergeant Villano. He would arrange for the beating. That's all I can tell you."

"One more thing," Joey responded. "Why did you have Manigrove killed?"

"I didn't," Doyle answered. "He was more interested in the illegal activities at the 8-8-5-2, than anything I was doing. I had every reason to leave him alone."

Joey stood up. "I am having you placed in the stockade at Fort Knox, where you will face a court-martial on charges of treason, dereliction of duty and conspiracy to have me killed." He closed the tape recorder. Picked it up and left the room.

Lieutenant Colonel Francis X. Doyle looked blankly at the wall ahead of him. He was content, but his pain was flaring up again.

22

ANOTHER KILLING

It was close to midnight when Joey returned to his motel room. He was tired yet exhilarated by the evening's events. Much had been accomplished, but much remained a mystery. Spies had been caught, but Captain Manigrove's death appeared to have no connection to the conspirators. Doyle had said something about the captain being interested in illegal activities at the 8-8-5-2. Did the traffickers in high-fidelity radios and televisions kill him? And if so, why? Why was Carmela "Gorgeous" Fortunato so willing to point the finger at her own operation by giving him a gang style beating?

As he opened the door to his room, he caught the red message light on his telephone blinking like an ominous warning from a distant tower. He was tempted with letting it blink until morning, but it pulled him reluctantly to its source. He pressed the message button; there were two messages—the first from Corporal Frank Marconi. "Master Sergeant this is Frank Marconi. I haven't been entirely forthright with you.

I've been too scared. I told Captain Manigrove this, and he got killed. There are two operations going on in the electronics lab, not one. The second is way beyond hi-fi stuff. Very technical. If you can meet me tomorrow, I will fill you in. Please get in touch. Bye."

The second message was a dark echo of the first. "This is for Master Sergeant Joey Klugman. This is First Sergeant Creighton Smith of the Military Police. A man has been found dead at the 8-8-5-2 Technical Service Unit. General Stockton has ordered you to proceed immediately to the scene and take charge."

It was close to one in the morning when Joey arrived at the secret unit. A somber guard Joey recognized as one of his beating saviors waved him in. He walked down the main street of the complex. It had lost its college quality. It looked more like a parade ground that had known thousands of boots. It sloped slightly, then leveled to abrupt flatness. Joey knew before seeing the body that it was Frank Marconi.

Corporal Frank Marconi looked like a broken doll, his head resting at an odd angle from his body. It appeared he had fallen from a second-floor window of the physiology building—the place where animal experimentation and dissection took place. "What was he doing here?" Joey asked the MP sergeant standing near the body.

"He was the NCOIC tonight and apparently was making his rounds of the buildings," the sergeant answered. "Maybe, he found a door open."

"Maybe," Joey said.

Joey looked up at the open second-floor window. "That's where he must have fallen from. What would he be doing up on the second floor?'

The sergeant shrugged.

Follow me, Sergeant," Klugman ordered.

The main door to the building was open, and the odor of death and disinfectant hit them as soon as they entered. Except for the pungent mix of cordite and burned flesh, the place had the stink of a battlefield, Joey thought. "But there won't be human bodies," ran hopefully through his mind as they climbed a flight of stairs. When they reached the second floor, they heard the barking of dogs and the chatter of monkeys and apes protesting their steel cages. "Experimental animals," Joey said. The death smell from down below mixed with the odor of dog food, decaying vegetables and shit on the second floor.

"Ugh," gasped the sergeant.

Using their flashlights, they made their way to the open window. A nearby cabinet had been knocked over. Some containers had broken, and their contents had spilled. A brown, gooey substance, released from a broken jar, slowly expanded across the wooden floor. "Maybe he put up a fight," the sergeant said.

"I don't think so," answered Joey. "But from the bruising I saw across the back of Corporal Marconi's neck, I bet it was broken right here. He probably fell against the cabinet before hitting the ground. He was thrown out the window to cover up what really killed him."

As they stood in the semi-darkness, Joey thought he smelled something else, something that shouldn't have been in the physiology building. "Do you smell that?" he asked the sergeant.

"Lots of dog poop and formaldehyde," the MP answered.

"No, something nice. I smell perfume," Joey responded.

"Perfume, here?" the sergeant sniffed. "Yeah, I do smell it. It's almost overwhelmed by the general stink, but there is definitely the smell of perfume here."

Joey remembered where he had noticed that scent before. It had surrounded Lieutenant Gorgeous in a diaphanous veil as she approached his table at *The Twelve Angry Men*. "That bitch killed my only witness," he said.

The MP sergeant looked at him blankly.

Back on the street, an officer was examining the body. As Joey approached, the officer looked up. "Captain Ted Feinman, I'm a forensic doctor with the CID," he said.

"I'm Master Sergeant Joey Klugman, a CID detective in charge of this case," Joey replied.

"I'm stationed at Fort Knox. I'm told you're out of Washington and report directly to General Stockton," Captain Feinman said.

"Something like that," Joey responded. "I would appreciate being apprised of your findings."

"You'll be the first to know," the captain answered. "Off the top, I can tell you this guy was struck a severe blow to the back of the neck—a karate chop that could have broken his spinal cord and caused instant death. But I'll know more after I autopsy him."

Joey nodded.

Feinman then added, "General Stockton's sergeant major wants you to call him as soon as possible."

Joey nodded his thanks and left Marconi in the hands of the captain. He walked briskly up the hill that led to unit's exit, stopping only when he got to the guard shack. He reached for the phone and dialed the sergeant major's desk at the headquarters building. To Joey's surprise, a voice answered on the first ring. "Sergeant Major Case, here," it said.

"Up a bit late, Sergeant Major," Joey responded. "This is Master Sergeant Klugman. I hope I wasn't keeping you up."

"Not exactly. But murder was. And the general would like you here and now to fill him in. And you can call me Corky."

"I'll be over in a minute," Joey responded and hung up.

It was close to 2:30 in the morning when Joey entered General Stockton's office. Stockton was clean shaven. His uniform crisp and tailored. His pearl-handled .38 glared a creamy whiteness in the fluorescence of the room. "Well?" he said.

"Sir, there has been a murder at the 8-8-5-2," Joey started.

"Damn. I know that. Tell me something I don't know. I've tried to locate that goddamn Doyle to get some understanding but can't find him."

"Yes, sir" Joey began. "We arrested Lieutenant Colonel Doyle a few hours ago in Louisville for spying.

He had just passed secret information to a Soviet agent when we grabbed him."

Stockton's look moved from anger to shock then back again. A flush began at his neck then traveled like so many pink fingers to rejoin on his cheeks. "Son of a bitch!" he exclaimed. "Who knows this? Why didn't you tell me?"

"I never had a chance, sir. The FBI blindsided me. They told me only when the arrest was about to be made. But we made the arrest together," Klugman answered.

"Bastards. Hoover wants the glory. Who have they told?" Stockton asked.

"I'm not sure," Joey shot back. "Just their immediate superiors, as far as I know."

"Then I may still be first in alerting the Pentagon," said the general. "Fill me in quickly, just the overview. You can put the details in your report."

Joey ran through the phone taps that led them from Jeffrey Wade to Vladimir Karpov to Doyle. Neither he nor the FBI agents had direct evidence against Wade, but all believed he was part of the ring.

"Well done," Klugman, the general finally said. "Corky!" he shouted into the intercom, "Get me Major General Cartwright at the Pentagon. Wake him at home if you have to."

Stockton turned back to Joey. "This will get you another goddamn medal," he said.

"The FBI agents did most of the work on this one, sir," Joey responded. "They deserve the credit."

"Bullshit," the general replied. "You were in charge. The CID was the lead agency. I don't give a damn about those civilians. Take what's yours."

He brought out a bottle of bourbon and poured a shot of Joey then himself.

Joey shrugged and drank. The burn down his throat felt good. To Stockton, this wasn't about security leaks. This was about credit. And blame. You rose on credit. You sank on blame. Word of the breach had reached the Secretary of Defense's office. If that breach was not secured, Stockton's career would be over. If it was secured by some agency not under his command, he would look incompetent to his superiors, someone who could not clean up the foulness in his own nest. He would never sit on the Joint Chiefs of Staff. But Doyle's arrest, the capture of a Soviet agent by someone under his command changed everything. The future was open.

"I have to get back to the case," Joey said, breaking Stockton's reverie.

Stockton stared up at him. "What case? Isn't it over? Oh, yes the dead man."

"Besides the spies, crooks have been operating out of the 8-8-5-2," Joey answered. "The dead man was going to fill me in. But someone got to him first. As you've heard, he was murdered."

Stockton looked at him blankly.

Joey then explained how a group of electrical engineers within the unit had gone into the business of producing high-quality stereo systems and televisions using equipment paid for by the government. "They bought the equipment under the guise of needing it for experimental work. Their equipment requests were never questioned nor audited because of the secret nature of their work.

Somehow, they got connected to the mob, probably through Lieutenant Fortunato, who handled the distribution and sale of the equipment."

"Good God," said Stockton, seeing his rising career suddenly curve downward under a morass of scandal. "Let's get those sons-of-bitches, Klugman. If you need any muscle just tell Corky. And if this goes bad, it's your ass and the ass of that colonel who sent you down here."

Joey ignored the general's remark. "And we still don't know who killed Captain Manigrove and Corporal Marconi.," he continued. "My guess is the captain and the corporal knew too much and were going to talk."

The general slumped in his chair. He looked worn, tired.

"Am I dismissed, General?" Joey asked.

Stockton looked up, again hard, tough. "Yes, you are dismissed. But just remember what I said about the asses that will get fried if this goes down badly," he said.

Even though he was in civilian clothes, he saluted, turned and left. Sergeant Major Case was still on the phone looking for General Cartwright at the Pentagon. He put his hand over the phone's mouthpiece and looked at Joey. "It's all about power, isn't it? That's why I never took a commission," he said.

"Me too, Corky," Joey answered and left into the dark night.

23

A GORGEOUS INVITATION

The world had a stark blackness to it as Joey walked to his car. In the distance, he could see the silhouette of several tanks. Somehow, they blended into one fierce dark mountain. He half expected a volcanic explosion that would send fire, red hot boulders and suffocating ash shooting skyward. It would be nature's demonstration of real, unstoppable power, the laughter of the gods at the inconsequential noises of an arrogant man.

But instead of a cataclysmic bang, he heard only a low, oddly accented voice that sounded vaguely familiar. "Get in the car and drive down to the 8-8-5-2," it said. The command was enforced by the barrel of a pistol shoved against Joey's spine.

"You're the gate guard," Joey exclaimed. "What the hell are you doing?"

"Just do as I tell you. Reach slowly into your jacket, and with two fingers slowly remove your weapon, and hold it over your head," the burly guard said. Joey did as he was told. The .38 was quickly snatched away. "Now drive to the 8-8-5-2."

Joey slipped into the driver's seat. The guard moved into the passenger seat behind him, pressing the .45 caliber's cold barrel against Joey's head. He started the engine, shifted into gear and slowly drove out of the parking lot and down the road to the 8-8-5-2. "What's your name soldier?" Joey asked.

"Just shut up and drive," the guard said. "I've heard enough of your talk."

"I read your nameplate," Joey went on, certain that the angrier or more frightened his captor got, the more likely he would make a mistake. "It's Franz something, isn't it? Yes, Franz Ludaniczech That's it. Ludaniczech. Interesting name. You fight in Korea?"

Franz Ludaniczech's face twisted into an ugly sneer. "I fought. I fought with the People's Republic of North Korea. I was there as a training officer. I killed plenty of you Americans. I should just blow you away. But they want to see you first. See how much you know. Then it will be my turn."

Joey was surprised. He recalled that Ludaniczech's file mentioned that he was among several hundred East European refugees who had volunteered for the army as a means to early citizenship. The military and the State Department had a program that allowed political refugees from behind the Iron Curtain to become citizens upon completion of a tour of duty. But he had never thought that a Soviet agent could be smuggled into the 8-8-5-2. "Probably the work of the good Colonel Karpov," Joey thought to himself. "Why hadn't I checked further on this guy?" Joey thought. "Dummy," his thoughts answered back.

As they approached the gate, Ludaniczech said, "Just show the guard your pass and drive on. Nothing clever."

Joey nodded. He flashed his pass as did his captor. Joey thought about suddenly exiting the vehicle, but another car pulled up behind, and the guard waved them through.

"Head down to the big building at the very end of the block," Ludaniczech snapped.

"What's there?" Joey asked.

"Just drive," the guard answered.

Joey shrugged his shoulders and drove slowly down the street, passed darkened buildings marked Electrical Engineering, Chemistry, Biology, Physiology and, finally, Experimental. Even in the dark, Joey could tell it was far bigger than the other structures. And unlike the other wooden buildings, this one was all steel and concrete. They entered through a side door. It took Joey several seconds to adjust to what had seemed utter blackness. He realized he was in a building about half the size of a football field. Small red lights illuminated hallways and signs over doors.

"Welcome, you son of a bitch," a velvety voice said. Lieutenant Gorgeous suddenly became visible. Even baggy fatigues could not conceal her well-proportioned body. She would have been a vision of loveliness, except for the pistol in her hand—and the man standing behind her.

"Get rid of the weapon and the jerk next to you, and you would be the girl of my dreams," Joey said. "That is you, Victor, isn't it? Hiding behind the little lady?"

"Not from you, Klugman," Victor Rodney snarled. "You are going to die."

"From electrical engineer, to lousy gambler, to thief and now to murderer. Now that's a career your folks can really be proud of," Joey answered. "Rich boy to total loser."

"I'm gonna spit on your body!" Rodney screamed and moved toward Joey.

"Bring it on man," Joey goaded. "People a lot tougher than you have tried to kill me. Ask your other shadowy buddy. That is you, Tony. No need to hide. You've got big Franz behind me. Gorgeous in front and wimpy Victor."

Tony stepped into view but said nothing.

Gorgeous laughed as Rodney began to move forward again. She grabbed his arm. "He's just trying to goad you, Victor," she said. "Now you and Tony go to the shaking machine and wait for us there. Franz and I will give the master sergeant a tour of our facilities."

"We better go with you," answered Tony. "I've seen this guy in action."

"Do what I tell you!" Carmela Fortunato shot back, her voice suddenly hard. "Franz will be quite enough."

"'Lick your balls, then tear out your heart,' isn't that the way you described the gorgeous lieutenant?" Joey quipped at Tony. "And why did that gorgeous, intelligent, well-educated piece of ass become a murderous bitch?" Joey asked, turning to Carmela.

"Ambition," she answered.

24

MORE THAN GORGEOUS

Carmela Fortunato was not made of sugar and spice and everything nice—though she looked like it. But inside that sugar candy gauze, beat a heart as ambitious and ruthless as it was cold and calculating. That is not to say she lacked a certain loyalty to her family, both immediate and extended. She was a member of the Lanteri crime family, whose head is Antonio Lanteri, noted Brooklyn Mafia Don.

Tony Lanteri was a suave, handsome man whose jet-black hair was laced with soft streaks of gray. He was five feet nine inches tall, squarely built with a thick chest and muscular arms. Women found him attractive. Men said he had a benign almost priestly face, which made his appearance a contradiction to his actions. At 56, he was at the top of his game. He controlled gambling, prostitution, loan sharking and the protection business in a wide swath of his borough of nearly three million. He was known as a man who rarely raised his voice or displayed anger. If he was opposed, he tried negotiation, bribes and a modulated violence to match the issue at hand. If all else failed, there was, of course, murder. He did not take this course of action lightly, but he considered it part of doing business in a very competitive environment. There was no venom in his murders. Revenge, he felt, was wasteful of resources, for it triggered retaliation. And retaliation fostered only more retaliation. Murder was the result only of failed negotiation.

His personal life did not run as rhythmically as his business operations. He had hoped for sons, who at some point would succeed him, but the Lord, in his wisdom, had left his wife, Rosa, barren. The Don had a problem. He craved orderliness and recognized that without a clear successor his final departure would leave his extended family in turmoil. The ambitious would rise up. Wars inevitably would follow. Lanteri was certain of this because in his quiet times he had read about the kings of England, hoping to learn from their mistakes. He admired the kings' skill in ruling and thus was profoundly aware of their difficulties in picking heirs to the throne.

The Don had looked toward his younger sister, Maria, for the male heir.

She had married Paolo Fortunato, a family soldier, but they had difficulties as well. A son died at birth. Then came their only child, Carmela—a hellcat, a fiery beauty with long claws and a sharp mind. She would have made a fine successor. But, alas, she was a woman. No woman could head a crime family. It was not a British realm. By tradition, by the physical facts of life, it was a man's job. No woman was physically strong enough. They were too easily seduced. They were softened too much by love.

He became intrigued by a fast-rising young tough named Anthony Villano. Tony had done some amateur boxing and had shown promise, winning a Golden Gloves lightweight championship and acquiring the nickname "Hits" for his rapid-fire on target punching. But President Street in Brooklyn was offering better pay for those capable of inflicting pain intelligently. The tools of his trade were no longer just his fists. Tony "Hits" quickly became skilled with lead pipes wrapped in newspapers, baseball bats, and tire irons. He advanced so quickly to shootings, knifings, and strangulations that the nickname "Hits" took on another, more threatening, meaning. The Don found him someone who could be counted on for swift, reliable work. No questions asked.

Something else about young Tony caught Lanteri's eye. He learned that Tony had graduated high school near the top of his class and was taking night courses at Brooklyn College. "Smart," thought the Don. "Tough and smart. I like that." The Don had always wanted to finish high school. He liked learning, but his parents were poor tailors. He had needed to go to work when he was sixteen.

Gradually, Lanteri brought young Tony directly under his wing. He became the Don's personal bodyguard. "We both were named after Saint Anthony," Lanteri told him. "That was like a sign from God. I want you close to me." Young Tony felt that he had somehow been blessed, if not by Saint Anthony at least by one of his angels. He went to church that same day and gave thanks to the Father, Son and Holy Spirit for showing him this kindness.

Tony Lanteri's attention to Anthony Villano did not go unnoticed by Carmela. She had known Villano since they were children. She had always found him cute, athletic, smart and respectful of her. He also had that depth of loyalty to her uncle that only she and a few others truly shared. She remembered him, even as a boy, saying that he would die for his Don, and she knew he meant it.

He also was ambitious. But unlike most of the others in the neighborhood, he recognized that the family business was changing. It was entering an era of respectability. Violence was not enough. Not only did money made the old way have to be laundered, but it also had to be utilized as an economic weapon. It was not enough to extort protection money from a dress manufacturer or be his loan shark—factor as they said in the trade—it was important to become his partner, to go legitimate. Money was merely a tool for power. Tony Villano saw night school at Brooklyn College as a means of understanding how to turn the old coin into the new.

Carmela had seen all this in Tony "Hits" as well. And she saw the future of the business in much the same way as he did. She had finished at the top of her class at Our Mother of Faith High School for Girls, and with her uncle's full support, she became the first in her family to attend college. Not just any college but Harstonia. The dons at this illustrious Ivy League university were fully aware of her lineage but decided that the addition of Carmela would add a unique diversity to the freshman class. They were more concerned that Mr. Antonio Lanteri might extend a certain generosity to the school and offer a building that would require his name. They understood he took rejection poorly. Uncle Tony, however, proved sophisticated enough to offer only a substantial anonymous donation, which was accepted.

Thus Tony "Hits" and Carmela were headed on a collision course. He was the anointed one, she the rightful heir.

But that did not become apparent until later. In their teens, Tony and Carmela were drawn to each other first by a shared passion, then by the instinctive understanding that they shared both intelligence and ambition. Tony "Hits" and Carmela first made love in an abandoned tenement apartment. He had asked her to come up to the roof of the building to share a view of the night sky and drink some beers that he had hidden behind a ventilator. They drank beer and looked at the stars.

"That's the North Star there, just out from the Big Dipper," he said.

"Where?" she asked, turning toward him and into his arms.

"Here," he replied, kissing her on the lips.

She kissed him back. He placed his tongue in her mouth and whispered,

"French kiss."

"Yes," she responded by searching his mouth with her tongue.

Tony placed a cautious hand on her breast. She responded with a sigh. He pressed her to him, dropping his hands to her firm buttocks. "Let's go downstairs. I know an empty apartment that's open," he said. She simply nodded.

Holding hands tightly, they made their way down darkened stairs to apartment 6 D. The door was open. The only light came from a bright moon. An old mattress lay on the floor in a corner of the bedroom. He pulled her toward it but not down. While they stood, he slowly unbuttoned her blouse. He put his arms around her and unhooked her bra. He clumsily held her naked breasts, one in each hand. Then he kissed each nipple. She moaned. He slid his hands to the zipper holding her skirt and pulled it down. She hadn't worn a slip. He slipped her panties down revealing a flat belly and a lush mound of black, curly hair. Carmela completed removing her clothes, and said, "Now you." He gasped in excitement.

As Tony opened his shirt, she opened the belt to his pants, unbuttoned the top button and slid the zipper down. She pushed his pants down to his ankles and looked at the bulge in his boxer shorts. She giggled, reached inside and drew out his stiff, pulsating cock. "I always wondered what they looked like," she whispered.

"You never seen one before?" Tony asked.

"Only my dad, and it wasn't stiff and fat like yours," she answered, still stroking his cock gently. "It has a curve. It's like a swan," she said.

Tony reached into her vagina, finding it wet and pliable. Suddenly she pushed him. His feet were still in his pants, and he fell awkwardly onto the mattress. Carmela laughed, pulled down his shorts and removed his pants, socks, and shoes. In one motion, she climbed on top of him and pushed his hard cock into her soft vagina. "Oh, God. Oh, sweet Jesus," Carmela cried as she began to rock back and forth, up and down on Tony's hot, oozing rod. He came, his body going rigid. He was somewhere between ecstasy and pain. He grunted, then relaxed. His heavy breathing slowed. He felt himself descend into the mattress. He suddenly became aware of the broken springs under its heavy quilting.

Carmela still straddled him. "I rode you like a pony," she said.

"You never rode a pony," Tony responded.

"You are my pony," she answered. "I want to ride you some more."

They remained lovers until Carmela left for Harstonia. There she met a young engineering student named Vincent Rodney. He was attending the prestigious Massachusetts Institute of Technology. He was bright, charming and came from one of the Blue Book American families. Carmela was fascinated and impressed. Someone from the upper, upper crust was interested in her. They became intimate for a time. But while Vincent liked this beautiful, little Italian girl, he loved gambling more. He was sure he could develop a mathematical system that would beat the table odds that always tilted toward the house.

Carmela, through her family connections, was able to bring him into the circle of professional gamblers that was protected by the mob. The games were held in private homes, usually those of women whose lovers had left them with a child but no financial support. They would supply food and drink throughout the night in exchange for a dollar or two from each hand played. They were not to flirt or distract the players in any way. The gamblers played for high table stakes, mostly poker, and often had backers who would frown on any undo connections between the house and the gamblers. However, until they turned to the mob for protection, their games frequently were robbed. There was lots of cash around, and the police were not an option because gambling was illegal. Mob muscle proved an expensive but acceptable form of insurance.

Vincent Rodney, however, pushed the boundaries of his luck too far. He lost $10,000 in the games, and when his family refused to pay, he turned to Carmela. She, in turn, called her uncle who made things right with the proviso that Vincent stop gambling. He did not and was soon back in debt.

"Stop him or I will," Antonio Lanteri told Carmela. The next night, as Vincent entered his apartment, he was surprised to see Carmela with two very large men. One walked up to him and punched him hard in the stomach. As he bent from the blow, the thug hit him crisply on the back with both hands. Rodney collapsed to the floor gasping for air. The second man then came up and kicked him hard in the ribs. The pain made Vincent cry. As he lay in a fetal position sobbing, Carmela kneeled and whispered, "If you ever cross me again, I'll have you killed." She and the two very large men left.

Vincent Rodney did not see Carmela again until he arrived at the 8-8-5-2.

25

MEN ONLY

Carmela's graduation from Harstonia University was cause for a great celebration for the Lanteri Crime Family. No member of their peculiar organization had ever graduated college and to have done so from the most prestigious university in the United States was an accomplishment beyond the dreams of most residents of President Street. "This is a great country," pronounced Antonio Lanteri. "We must have a party, a great party."

On a hot Sunday in July, traffic on a two-block section of President Street was blocked off from traffic and festooned with streams of multi-colored lights. Vendors rolled carts filled with the foods of southern Italy down the hot pavement. It was free—hot and sweet sausage, calamari, gelato, swollen ripe figs and dolce of all kinds. Small freezers, filled with dry ice, dispensed limoncello and other alcoholic digestives.

The Sun brightened the street, but a light breeze funneled cool air through the channel formed by

the parallel walls of brown tenements. Police estimated the joyful, milling crowd at over 300. Carmela was
driven through the street, seated on the back of
a white Cadillac convertible. Uncle Tony and Carmela's parents shared the back seat. Tony "Hits"
drove. The heavily built "Fat" Artie Regina rode in
the shotgun seat. A Beretta pistol rested in his lap.
Tony "Hits" weapon was tucked under his seat. It
never hurt to take precautions.

Toward evening, the Don's inner circle moved
to Giovanni's Restaurant, a small but elegant eating
place known for its vitello and dolce—veal chops
and desserts. Giovanni announced to his guests
that "Tonight, the meal is on me." There was hap-
piness everywhere. Carmela had come home.

After dessert, espressos, and digestives, the
Don stood up and bowed to Carmela. "I have
great plans for this young woman. She will be taking over the family's finances. We need someone
with a good head to do our books and make our
investments. In other words, to make our figures
look like her figure-great. The Don laughed at his
wit. Others laughed as well. Tony "Hits" looked
down and blushed.

"Our current financial adviser, my dear friend
Gino is retiring." In truth, Gino had not intended to
retire. The announcement came as news to him, but
he nodded with a stiff smile suggesting he had been
alerted. There could be no arguing. A decision had
been reached. He would abide. Lanteri had felt for
some time that Gino was good at hoarding money but not investing it. In the modern world, money must work for you. It was a concept Gino could

not grasp. He did not trust banks. In the old days, he robbed them. In Gino's mind, investment firms were run by slick Jews who promised more than they could ever deliver. Better to stick with the old ways: put the cash in the safe and have Vinnie "The Snake" guard it against unauthorized withdrawals.

Carmela, like Gino, smiled. And she, like Gino, was prepared to accept what her uncle declared. But there was a catch. And when the festivities ebbed, she asked the Don whether they could adjourn to his office for a talk. The wine had made Lanteri mellow. "Of course," he said in his gentle voice.

Lanteri's office was located a short walk from Giovanni's. The old man walked slightly ahead of Carmela, his two bodyguards slightly ahead. Carmela, as was her custom when walking with her uncle, removed the snub-nosed .32 caliber pistol from her purse and cupped it in her hand. The Don was protected.

The office entrance was drab. It announced itself in a small sign as the Assured Blue Stone Company, a wholesaler of crushed rock for roads and highways. No job was too small or too big. All work guaranteed. On a business day, pudgy Lena Calabrese sat behind a desk in a shabby foyer, screening those who wished to do business with Mr. Lanteri. If entrance were approved, the visitor would enter a dark, elegant room filled with rich oak furniture. Heavy curtains hung over barred and screened windows. A thick, soft, travertine colored carpet covered the floor. The light was subtle, discrete and controlled by a panel on Lanteri's large, rounded desk.

The Don took his seat behind the desk, in a thick, black leather chair that rocked and swiveled at the discretion of the occupant. Carmela sat before him the hard-backed chair reserved for supplicants. "What is it you want?" Lanteri asked in his avuncular voice.

"One day, I want to sit in your chair," Carmela responded firmly.

For a moment, Lanteri was silent. Then he smiled and said, "You don't have the balls for it." He laughed at his own humor.

"I am tougher than any of those cafones you have around, and I'm ten times smarter," she replied.

"Smarter, yeah. You are a lot smarter. That's why I am putting you in charge of the money. But tougher? I don't think so. You have got to have no heart to run this business. When you deal and compete with guys who would cut your throat, you have got to have no feelings about cutting theirs. No woman, not even you, can think that way. God made women to be soft in their hearts, to love, have sympathy, be caring. Men need that. Men need women the way they are, so that they can keep men in balance. No one can change what God has created." The Don had finished and began to rise.

"I'm not done," Carmela snapped her voice coal black in anger. "Sit."

Lanteri hesitated. He loved this woman as if she were his own daughter. If only she had been a man, he thought, she could have been his successor. Now she commands me to sit. Now she insults me. He continued to rise from his chair. "Meeting is over," he said.

"The hell it is, Uncle," Carmela replied. She had pulled the small automatic from her purse and aimed it at the Don. "Sit."

He looked at the weapon and then at her eyes, measuring whether she would really pull the trigger. Her hand did not quiver. Her eyes did not blink. They were cold and dark. He dropped back in his chair. "I think you would shoot me," he said.

"Now you have done two things. One very good. The other very bad," he continued. "You showed me you are willing to gamble your life to get what you want. And that's good. But you also have shown your disloyalty to me after all I have done for you. And that is bad. And for that, you will be punished. I want you off the street by tonight. You are no longer a member of the family. If you show your face in our territory, I will have you killed. I am sorry for this, but you leave me no choice. No one talks to a head of a family this way. No one, man or woman, threatens a Capo with death and gets away with it. If you weren't of my blood, I would have you killed now."

A deep red had climbed from below his neck and crept to his cheeks. No one had ever angered him this much. Perhaps it was because he cared for her that she was able to reach him in this way. He was not done. "Never, never since the Mafia was born. Never in all the times we were bandits, guerrilla fighters against the French, murderers and, yes, Robin Hoods. Never since we were known as the Cosa Nostra have we had a woman as a leader. It is not part of our history, not part of our tradition. This was always a man's thing. And I will not be the one to change that. I will not be the one to bring dishonor upon 150 years of history. I will not shame myself. Now, go."

Carmela rose and slipped the automatic back in her purse. She was no longer angry. She saw through this male thing. It was a way to keep women down, in their place. "You are a hypocrite, Uncle. All your talk about the family being a business. No death, no violence is done for personal reasons. Yet now you choose not what is best for the family but what is best for your man's ego. It has always been that way with you and the other old men. Sons are worth more than daughters. Daughters are nothing. I am nothing. I shall go, not because you threaten me but because I must grow in my own way. I have a right to this, to become what I can become. I will not bring disgrace to the family. I will enrich it. You will see." With that, she walked passed him and into the night.

26

ARMY TIMES

Carmela was unsure how she left President Street, but she knew precisely where she wanted to go— an army recruiting station. A recruiter had talked to a gathering of women students on the Harstonia campus about career opportunities in the Women's Army Corps. The Corps was formed during World War II as a separate branch of the United States Army. Its members filled all non-combatant roles. Now with the Korean War in its second bloody year, women were again vitally needed to free up men for combat.

"You bright, college women can become officers and fill critical positions in this new army," the recruiter had told them.

One of the bright college women, Carmela recalled, had raised her hand and asked: "How come the army is integrating Negroes into all army units, including the infantry, but what you are offering us is a separate but equal deal?"

The recruiter smiled. He was a young officer with several rows of medals on his crisp uniform.

Carmela expected him to say something about women having their place, but they can't be mixed with men or put in combat where they could not just be killed. Worse they could be raped. Those North Koreans and Chinese would just love to get their hands on white women, she thought. But he didn't say that.

"You are right. The military is not yet ready to integrate women. The army is in many ways like every big business in the United States. Women are allowed to go just so far and no farther. But the army is different. It is a direct part of the government of the United States and must obey all the civil rights and human rights legislation passed by the Congress and approved by the President. It can't go to court and fight the government's laws and regulations. I think the time is coming when women will be fully integrated into the armed forces. And women like you can help make this possible. There are men like me who want to see this happen. We are missing out on an awful lot of brain power and skill by not offering you equal opportunities, but in the military, you will find more equality than in the private sector. I urge you to join and make this transition quicker and easier."

As much as she liked what the recruiter said, Carmela had other fish to fry. She wanted a high office in the Mafia, not the army. But now that her uncle had excommunicated her from the family, the army might be the way to go. Ordinary business wasn't for her. Besides, she liked weapons.

Carmela breezed through basic training, demonstrating an outstanding ability with a variety of firearms, from bayonets to rapid firing Browning Automatic Rifles. Handguns were her real specialty, qualifying as an expert both with a .45 caliber Browning pistol and a .38 caliber revolver. She performed equally well on the academic tests required by the service and graduated Officer Candidate School with honors. Shortly after gaining the gold bars of a second lieutenant, she was assigned to the 8-8-5-2 Technical Service Unit.

Her first meeting with Lieutenant Colonel Francis X. Doyle astounded her. This tall, gaunt man stood as she entered his office and gave her a courtly bow. She saluted, not knowing how else to respond. It was no accident that she was assigned to the 8-8-5-2, he told her. He had requested someone outstandingly bright to deal with a platoon of brilliant, mostly immature, young men. It would be a difficult assignment because most had been drafted into a military with which they wanted no part. If not for fear of arrest, most of them would have fled by now.

"I did not know you were such a beautiful, young woman," he told her. "I am not sure whether that will make your job as my chief aide harder or easier." It was a calculated evaluation. He was a man determining pluses and minuses just as her uncle had done many times. She also sensed that the lieutenant colonel was attracted to her. She immediately knew that she could manipulate him. And there was something likable about him as well. The boy geniuses would be easy. They would stare at her face, then her breasts, then her ass and do whatever she asked.

Over time, Carmela recognized that Doyle was in great pain, both physically and emotionally. She offered herself to him because she felt something unique for her—compassion. He cared deeply about his work, and he cared about the people it would affect.

But sometimes the physical and emotional pain became too much for him. One morning she found him doubled over in his chair. Without a word, she pulled him to his feet and hugged him with all her strength, somehow seeking to force the pain out of him.

Slowly, she moved her hand down and gently rubbed his genitals. She felt him rise and then recede. "I can't," he whispered. "Ever since the radiation, I can't." Filled with emotions he had not felt since the death of his wife, he then revealed that he was giving certain of the nation's secrets to the Soviets. "For money?" she had asked. "No, for humanity," he responded.

This Doyle didn't simply love America. He loved the whole world. Giving the Russians secrets in the belief he was saving humanity was crazy. She knew men in power did not work that way. Yet the more she spent time with him, the more she admired him. "Don Quixote in a white coat," she thought.

She told him she wanted no part of giving away secrets unless there was money involved in it. Since there was none, there was no reason to face jail or perhaps a firing squad. But she would keep his treason secret and would give him cover if he would help her in a little private enterprise. Carmela had found Victor Rodney working in the electronics lab.

Her old boyfriend was torn between lust and fear when they met on the main street of the 8-8-5-2. She looked great in taut fatigues, but the thought of the two Boston thugs wracked his brain, which said: "Run!"

But Carmela put him at ease. "Let bygones be bygones," she said. They met at *The Twelve Angry Men* where, in a dark corner, she kissed him tenderly. "See, all better," she said. "You are gorgeous," he whispered back groping for her thigh. Carmela kept his hand from moving too far. She knew how to use her sex to arouse and control men. With Victor Rodney, it was easy.

He soon told her that he was still into gambling, that he had run up some big debts in Louisville but that he and a couple of other electronics guys at the 8-8-5-2 were making ends meet by assembling and selling a few high-fidelity radios and television sets using government parts. The sales were mostly to personnel at the fort.

"If I expanded your customer base, say to Louisville and beyond, could you increase capacity?" she asked.

"Maybe," he responded, "But if we requisition too many of the same parts, Colonel Doyle might get suspicious. He goes over the requisition lists personally."

"Don't worry, now I go over the requisition lists for him," she answered. Rodney looked at her suspiciously. "You got something going with Doyle?" he asked. Carmela smiled, put a finger to her lips and whispered. "Shh." Rodney shook his head. "There's another problem," he went on, "We've got no way to move things out of the fort."

"I have a way," Carmela replied. The way was Tony "Hits."

Carmela had not found Tony. He had found her. He was waiting just outside the 8-8-5-2. "Carmela," he said, "The saints have sent you to me."

"The saints or my uncle?" she replied, wondering if Tony would now gut her with the long switch blade he always carried.

"Trust me, the saints. The Don has no idea where you are. But he still cares about you. And I would never hurt you."

"Maybe," she answered, "but the Don doesn't care for me enough to let me run the family. I am the best for the job, even better than you."

"It doesn't matter what I think. No woman can have it. The family wouldn't accept a woman, and sure as hell, the other capos wouldn't. Leave it at that."

Logically, Carmela knew Tony was right. But this was the 1950s, and things could change. Elvis Presley was changing music; the Kinsey Report was changing the way Americans looked at sex; the pill had arrived, and a woman named Margaret Sanger was openly preaching birth control; Tennessee Williams was writing plays that told the truth about men and women, and rebel actors like Marlon Brando and James Dean were saying "Fuck you" to the world. Nothing had changed yet on President Street, but she could make it change. She would have shot her uncle if it would have brought change, but the men were not ready for it. She would have to persuade, negotiate and, if necessary, kill.

During the past two years, she had cut off all communication with the family. She neither wrote nor called her mother or father, though she missed them. She knew that they would tell her uncle, and he might do something. She, after all, had insulted him. She had talked to him like no one would have dared who wanted to stay alive. She hated that moment and enjoyed it as well. She respected the Don, but she was not afraid of him.

"So, what are you doing here, and how did you find me?" she asked Tony "Hits."

"I was drafted into the fucking army. Your uncle tried to pull some strings. I got doctors to say I was blind. I told them I had a rap sheet. Shit. It didn't matter. They sent me to Whitehall Street, where some doctor grabbed my balls, looked up my ass and said, 'You're fine. You got a record? What record? I don't see it in your folder.' The next thing I know, I'm in Korea, where a million fucking Chinese and Koreans are trying to kill me. They shot the crap out of me, but they couldn't kill this skinny Guinea. The joke was some Jewish guy came up and saved my ass just as some chink was putting a final hit on me. I spent five months in the hospital and then was assigned to Knox. I did a few deals here and got busted by the MPs, but they got nothing. I'm going to beat the rap, go home and make a ton of money."

"To answer your second question, word got out that some gorgeous, dark-haired broad with a great ass and tits was working out of the secret unit that nobody is supposed to know about, but everybody does. I knew it had to be you."

Carmela laughed. It had been a while since she laughed. She had worked hard in the army. She had avoided a social life. She had not been in the mood for anything beyond her daily work and reading to expand her mind. It kept her away from the groping hands of men. Men who thought they owned the world. Men, who thought women only good enough for bed, kids and doing the wash. But Tony "Hits" made her laugh again. She had missed him. He had not only been her lover but a good friend. He was handsome in an Italian way. She liked that. He was smart, the rare college man in the mob. But he had not let college rob him of his ruthlessness. She liked that too. He respected her, unlike most men. And she liked that as well.

They spent the first night after they met at a small motel, several miles from the fort.

They made love with the familiarity of long-time lovers, touching, caressing each other with gentle affection. When he entered her, she moaned, pulled hard on his neck and kissed him deeply.

Finally spent, they talked. Tony told her about the ring of thieves he had put together, involving a number of cooks, PX employees and guys from the motor pool. They were supplying Louisville restaurants with cut-rate food, cigarettes, and cigars. Clothing, shaving gear, over the counter medicines and toiletries went to local supermarkets. "No big deal but a living," he told her. He had come under suspicion, which had delayed his discharge. "But they can't prove a thing," he told her.

Then she told him about Victor Rodney and the wholesale radios and televisions. "If you can get me trucks to move the merchandise to Louisville, I can turn Victor's operation into a real moneymaker.

But this is my thing. You do this my way. You listen to me."

"Hey, if I can make a buck, I listen to you," he said. He laughed and slapped her naked ass lightly.

"One other thing," she said. "We send a percentage back to the Don."

"From us?" Tony asked.

"From me," Carmela replied and kissed him softly on the lips.

Tony shrugged and smiled. He knew no matter what she sent the Don, it would make no difference. It was unfair, but that was life. "Life doesn't have to be fair. It just has to be," he thought. In bed, he happily followed her lead. There, he enjoyed sharing their experiences as equal partners. Afterward, he acknowledged that she was smarter than him, smart enough for him to follow personally. "Anything you want to send the Don as his cut is fine," he told her.

The enterprise came together a few days later at *The Twelve Angry Men*. Carmela arrived with Victor. "This is a bad guy place," Victor said, recalling conversations with some of his gambling associates.

"Did you forget? I'm a bad girl," Carmela answered casually. With that, she led him to the end of the lengthy bar and approached a man sipping a beer. "Victor, meet a friend of mine from my old neighborhood in Brooklyn, Tony, Tony Villano." She had decided that introducing him as Tony "Hits" might send the wrong message to a man who had once been worked over.

27

BIG DEAL

Captain Albert Ruppert Manigrove III felt supremely confident that fate had at last dealt him a winning hand. Yes, that stunted jackass of a general, Stockton, had sent him into this rat hole of weirdos and maniacs to look for spies. Instead of spies, he had found a band of thieves with bravado and a willingness to share when he confronted them. The choice, he had told them was simple. Cut him in or get turned in. They seemed more than amenable and said they would pay him a bit more if he would convey their weekly proceeds to a certain Johnnie Getch, known to his associates as "No Hand" Getch could be found at *The Twelve Angry Men*.

The first time he met Getch it was unnerving. He entered *The Twelve Angry Men* dressed in civilian clothes about one in the afternoon, figuring the lunch crowd would still be there. Much of it still was. He had lived long enough to know you never meet strangers alone in dark, unfamiliar places. He also took the precaution of tucking a .45 into a holster hidden under his jacket. The thug who served him a bourbon and branch water at the bar eyed him suspiciously when he asked for Mr. Getch.

"You mean Johnnie 'No Hand'?" he asked

"I do believe that is the same gentleman," Manigrove responded in the courtly family manner he had been taught.

"Why would he want to see you?" the bartender asked.

"Because if he doesn't, I will blow an apple sized hole through this bar and through you, sir, with the .45 I am pressing against your lovely leather upholstery." Manigrove had not removed his weapon from its holster, but he accompanied his threat with a menacing smile that warned the bartender not to gamble.

The thug hesitated for just a moment, then pushed a button. A door opened from a nearly black corner of the room, freeing a rectangle of yellow light. Centered in the doorway was a dark-haired man of average height with a mid-day five-o'clock shadow. He seemed well proportioned and almost youthful, perhaps in his late 30s. What unnerved Manigrove was that instead of a right hand, he had a steel claw, whose points appeared razor sharp. The bartender nodded slightly toward the captain, then quickly moved away.

"You looking for me?" Johnnie "No Hand" asked in a soft, almost musical voice.

"Yes sir, I am, as a humble messenger for Ms. Carmela Fortunato," Manigrove replied with a graceful bow and a careful eye on the claw.

"You queer?" "No Hand" asked.

"No sir, but I am armed. And I do resent the inquiry into my sexual preferences.

"Are you soliciting me?" Manigrove countered.

The claw swung back and forth, its blades opening and closing like living things. Angry, Getch said nothing for several seconds, then ignored the insult. He replied, "What's the message from Carmela?"

"It's not so much a message as a package," Manigrove answered. With that, he started to pull out the envelope containing $5,000.

"Not here!" "No Hand" snapped. "Follow me."

Manigrove strode two steps behind Getch to ensure he would not be struck by the back swing of the claw. They entered the almost invisible room. "No Hand" moved behind a desk and said, "Drop the package here. And don't move. I know what to expect. The numbers better come out right. With a surprising deftness for a one-handed man, Getch counted the cash while Manigrove fidgeted. He wondered whether he could get his pistol out before "No Hand" struck him with his claw. The claw's blades, he noticed, gently held a side of each bill as it was counted. "Plenty of practice," Manigrove thought. Finally, Getch said, "Five grand, the right number."

Then he looked up at Manigrove. "Hey, Mr. Fancy Moves, I'm going to show you what would happen if the count ever comes up with the wrong number." Manigrove moved a step back from the desk, his hand yanking out the .45.

Getch looked at him and laughed. "No need for the cannon. Nobody hurts anybody as long as we all play fair. If you don't play fair, well . . . "His voice trailed off as he walked to a second door in the room and beckoned with his claw for Manigrove to stand next to him. "No Hand" opened the door. Immediately, an ear-splitting roar filled the air. An incredulous Manigrove looked down a flight of stairs into the cold yellow eyes of a full-grown lion. It was restrained by a thick, steel chain attached to a collar around its neck. Manigrove was transfixed by the huge teeth and claws—and the stench of its breath and droppings. "Guys who cheat us become dinner for Vincenzo," "No Hand" said with a laugh.

Manigrove regained his composure, stepped back from the door and holstered his weapon. "Amusing, sir, very amusing," he said. "But you may be assured I will not cheat you. Members of my family have been known to steal but never to cheat.

"No Hand" looked back at him as he closed the door. "Members of my family have done both. That's why we got the lion."

Manigrove left *The Twelve Angry Men* shaken but not demoralized. "Just theater," he thought. "No Hand's" claw and the lion and the thugs. He had experienced war but nothing quite like this. Dealing with organized mobsters would take a bit of getting used to.

Over the months, he made numerous deliveries, all uneventful. In time, he became accustomed to dealing with "No Hand" Getch, Vincenzo the lion, and the crowd behind the bar.

One afternoon, after a delivery, Johnnie "No Hand" asked Manigrove if he would stay for a drink.

"I'd be delighted, sir, as long as the lion will not be with us," the captain said, bowing from the waist.

"No Hand" reached into his desk drawer and pulled out a bottle of expensive bourbon. "You Southern types like this stuff," he said. "It's not half bad, once you get used to it."

"It's like a Southern gentleman," Manigrove replied, "fine spirited and well-mannered but mean and unforgiving if put upon."

"You know, I like the way you talk," "No Hand" answered. "You got family? Kin?"

"I come from a very large family, Mr. Getch. It goes back several hundred years in this country," Manigrove responded. "Have you heard of Lafitte, the Pirate? He was a Manigrove who prowled the seven seas finding treasure, a noble brigand but one who always sent the family its due share. The family in turn always assured him a safe haven for his ship and a warm bed for his body. When he retired, the family assured him wealth for the rest of his life. We have been honest merchants as well—trafficking in everything from ivory to tobacco to rice and indigo."

"No slaves?" "No Hand" asked.

"We had them, but we did not traffic in them," Manigrove answered. "Two things we shunned: slavery, as a crime against the human soul and treachery to our country, which gave us freedom from persecution. And you, Mr. Getch, tell me about your family."

"No Hand" smiled. "You know all about my family. You might call it an extended family. We got the Capones, the Gambinos, the Lucianos and the Lanteris and lots more. My people mostly come from the poor part of Italy. My folks were from Sicily, where this thing, we call it our thing, started. They came to this country because otherwise, they would have starved to death. And when they came here, they find that people already here hated them. They hated them because they were poor and ignorant and spoke funny and were Catholics."

"That's funny in a way," Manigrove said. "My ancestors, who were French, were persecuted because they weren't Catholic."

"Life's a funny thing," "No Hand" answered.

"Since we're on the subject of funny things, perhaps you would be willing to share with me how you lost your hand?" asked Manigrove. He knew he might be touching a sensitive subject, but the bourbon gave him uncustomary courage.

"A grenade," said Getch.

"You saw combat?" Manigrove asked with surprise.

"Nothing like that," answered Getch. "I tossed a grenade at a laundry-mat whose owner didn't want to buy insurance from us, but I threw it too hard. It bounced back. I picked it up, and it exploded."

Manigrove instinctively grimaced. It reminded him of his war wound. But he said nothing.

"It all turned out okay, though," "No Hand" continued. "I sued the city for negligence. I claimed I had picked up a box on a city sidewalk, and it went boom. I collected fifty G's with no trial. The city settled. No trial, no nothing. New York City is wonderful."

Manigrove pondered whether he should move to the wonderful City of New York, sighed and recognized, he was too much a son of the South.

"And the claw?" he asked.

"Mostly, I use it to cut food," "No Hand" responded, then changed the subject.

"You've been straight with us," he continued. "No skimming a few bucks. Deliveries always on time. We like that. We appreciate that. But now something big is going down. We are going to make a big score, the kind of money you can't bring to *The Twelve Angry Men*. The local cops are watching us. And we think the feds are watching us. This next delivery won't go to me. You are going to take it to Grand Central Station in New York City, where a guy named Frankie "Fats" will meet you. You wear your uniform. You stand by the booth with all the train information. He'll find you."

"An interesting proposal, Mr. Getch," Manigrove replied. "And one I would be very interested in accepting, provided . . . " He paused, then continued. "I presume I would be substantially reimbursed for the additional risks and expenses."

"No problem. We will also get you laid by some of the most exquisite broads in the city," "No Hand" answered, enjoying the idea of sealing the deal with a bit of wild sex.

"I am sure I will find that highly entertaining," Manigrove answered. "But getting back to our proposition, first, how much money would I be carrying?"

"Minimum delivery $100, 000," Getch responded. "You are in for five percent plus expenses."

Manigrove's eyes widened, and he whistled softly. "That, my dear Mr. 'No Hand,' is a considerable sum and a generous offer." He thought for a moment about the inherent dangers of delivering such an amount of cash. Clearly, the source was illegal, so one or more law enforcement agencies could be after him. He also would be the potential target of any criminal who became aware of what he was carrying. Finally, this could be a setup, some scheme to make him a fall guy in an internal gang war. But after weighing the risks against the rewards, Manigrove said, "I accept, under certain conditions. First, the money is to be counted jointly by Lieutenant Fortunato and me before I assume responsibility for it. Second, I take my percentage before leaving. Third, Mr. Frankie "Fats" would have to know precisely how much was to be turned over to him. I wouldn't want to be accused of short-changing anyone."

Then he added, "I have two other questions. Who potentially would be coming after me? And what activity has generated this kind of money? There are some things I do not do, like being involved in any aspect of dope smuggling or white slavery."

"No Hand" made a face. "You can have your money count. Only the feds would be after you. And I can tell you this money does not come from drugs, white slavery or whores. But where it comes from is none of your fucking business."

28

CHIP TROUBLE

Captain Albert Ruppert Manigrove III pondered his lucrative new assignment as he drove away from *The Twelve Angry Men*. The money he would be moving was substantial. His percentage would enable him to send a creditable amount of money to the Manigrove Fund and keep enough to hand-somely handle his immediate needs.

Under the Manigrove system of monetary distri-bution, a financial account was established for each member as he or she was born. Sums would be deposited periodically, the individual amounts de-termined by a trio of elders. Their dictum preceded the Communist Manifesto but was substantially the same. Each member gave in accordance to his or her abilities. Each member received in accordance to his or her needs. Members could draw an annual percentage from their accounts. And at age 35 could administer their accounts as they saw fit.

If a member contributed fifty percent beyond the amount established as a personal minimum by the trio, ten percent of the windfall would be placed in a special Golden Account and become part of a highly speculative Manigrove investment fund. A contributor would receive a proportional return from the fund's usually substantial profits, which would be deposited directly into the contributor's account.

In addition, the name of each contributor to the Golden Account would be placed on The Directory of Success, which was located prominently in the family estate's library. Since the trio set high expectations for family contributors, it was difficult to achieve a place on The Directory of Success. Only thirty-two names were affixed to the directory since it was established in 1650. "What a great honor it would be to have my name on that list," Captain Albert Ruppert Manigrove III thought as he drove. His military pay had barely qualified him as a contributor, even with those little extra-curricular deals. "A $100,000 contribution would place me among the clan's elite," he thought. "But stealing from the mob would be unethical, more importantly, downright dangerous."

Then it occurred to Manigrove that he might reach a more reasoned conclusion if he could learn the source of the mob's new-found income. And who better to ask than honest, decent Frank Marconi. He caught up with the corporal as he sat under a big oak tree sipping coffee and reading a book. Manigrove caught the title as he approached, *Theoretical Physics.*

"Dull reading on a bright, sunny day," the captain exclaimed.

Marconi jumped to his feet and saluted. "I'm on my 10-minute break, sir," wanting to assure his superior that he was not derelict in his duty. "The book is supplemental educational reading. Its principles help in carrying out electronic engineering experiments."

Manigrove looked at the shorter Marconi for a moment, pondering why he probably was the only enlisted man in this entire unit that cared about dereliction of duty and respect for military rank. He returned the salute and said, "At ease, Soldier. I have a question, a security question. Is anything more unusual going on than what we have already talked about?"

Marconi's soft, brown eyes suddenly grew hard and dark. He also took a step closer to the big oak, leaning against it for support, perhaps strength. "I don't think so, sir," he said. "I should be going back to the lab. My break time is over."

"I'll get you excused," the captain said.

"That would only get me in more trouble," the corporal answered.

"I fully understand. We will meet after work outside the Officers Club at 1900 hours. That's an order, Corporal," Manigrove responded with all the authority he could muster.

"Yes, sir," Marconi said in defeat.

It was precisely at 1900 hours when Marconi approached him near the entrance to the Officers Club. He appeared to come out of the shadows, showing more stealth than Manigrove believed possible from such a chubby build. But fear put a certain edge to the corporal's behavior. He had seen that same unexpected sharpness in combat. Fear, he thought, seemed to ignite all of a man's senses. He recognized that he too was edgy, on guard, sharp. Was somebody following him? He took a quick look behind him, nothing but a couple of drunken majors and more shadows. And, yet . . .

He turned back to Marconi. "Again, Corporal, have you noticed anything more unusual than we have already talked about?" he asked.

"If there was, why should I tell you, sir?" Marconi snapped showing a belligerence that again surprised Manigrove. "You have done nothing with the information I gave you. In fact, they are making more TVs and Hi-Fi sets than ever before."

Manigrove put a conspiratorial tone in his voice and whispered, "Come closer, young man. And let me explain how this detective business works. Just because you handed me a piece of the puzzle doesn't mean I have the whole puzzle. I have been diligently putting together the whole network— from supply to manufacturing to distribution. That has taken time. I have been infiltrating them to their highest levels. Soon, I will be able to call in the MPs and arrest them all, top to bottom. But now I suddenly hear that they have somehow increased their profits tenfold. And it seems to have happened virtually overnight. I clearly have missed something big. Now, tell me what is going on, so I can put even more of them behind bars."

The captain's Southern drawl had sounded more and more sing song, almost incomprehensible to Marconi's New York ear, as the whispering went on. "Okay, okay," Marconi replied in a voice that both men knew was too loud.

"I think they have made a deal to develop something called an integrated circuit for the Russians. It has a lot to do with making computers work faster and cheaper," Marconi said. "They've told us, it's for a U.S. military computer system, but we are using a totally different approach. And only the Russians would need this kind of technology."

"Computers?" Manigrove responded. He had vaguely heard of these devices as some kind of very fast adding machines that the British had used to help break German codes during World War II. "Why would the Russians want to spend so much money to make faster adding machines?" he asked. "And why not use their own scientists?"

"Computers are the future, sir" Marconi answered. "And we are way ahead of them.

"Explain," Manigrove demanded.

"Computers were invented to solve complex equations that would take us hours or days or months or even years to solve," Marconi began. "This has tremendous military significance. For one thing, it allows us to calculate the trajectory of a long-range rocket with great accuracy. Remember the Germans were able to fire such rockets at Great Britain but had no real idea where they would fall. If they had computers, they could have made those rockets extremely accurate. Most of our computing is done with batches of specially punched cards, something like what train conductors do to your ticket when you get on board. Our military has been seeking to go past the cards by developing a so-called micromodule. But the Soviets are looking for another way, an even faster way involving solid circuits. I've read some of their journals. I think they are working on intercontinental missiles, weapons that could go from the heart of the Soviet Union to the heart of the United States."

"So why don't they use their scientists?" Manigrove asked.

"I don't know. My guess is that we are way ahead of them with this technology," Marconi answered.

Manigrove's mind immediately made the connections. "So, what you are telling me is that Russkies have hired our scientists, through the mob, to help them build a better way to bomb us."

"Yes," the corporal replied. "I don't know about the mob. But Victor Rodney assigns the work. He's asked me twice to participate. I won't, so now he has threatened me. I could end up looking like one of those dissected monkeys, he told me. I'm scared, Captain."

Manigrove put a fatherly arm around the worried corporal and told him not to worry. Now that he had revealed everything, the army would protect him and put all those thieves, spies and traitors in jail. Only slightly reassured, Corporal Frank Marconi turned and disappeared into the shadows.

Manigrove also felt uneasy. He had much to think about. With the Soviets as paymasters, the flow of funds could be inexhaustible. His cut could make him, and the Manigrove clan, wealthier than he could have imagined. Yet, this was treason. Flat out betrayal. Those idiot savant scientists in that electronics lab didn't know it—except for poor Marconi.

For them, it was simply an extra challenge, another puzzle to solve with solid scientific thinking. They got some extra money for their efforts as well. The mob could care less where the money came from. It was beyond their thinking to conceive of an American-designed computer guiding a Soviet nuclear warhead squarely into mid-town Manhattan, and that they would have contributed to their own demise. Oh, how the Russians would laugh. The Americans brought down by their own capitalist greed. Everything for a buck, even placing ourselves in our own graves.

Then it became clear. A Manigrove would do almost anything to turn a profit but not betray his country. This land that had given each of them freedom and opportunity could never be dealt away for a few pieces of silver. Certainly, Albert Ruppert Manigrove III would not be the first to defile this bargain. Then it came to him. He could be a patriot and make a profit at the same time. He smiled to himself and began to walk back to the Officers Quarters.

Perhaps it was the snap of a twig that caused Manigrove to turn. He could see nothing. He was edgy, he thought. A great enterprise was about to get under way. He turned back toward his quarters. A door to the Officers Club opened, throwing a sliver of yellow light against the figure of Tony "Hits" Villano. He quietly moved away.

29

SHAKE, SHAKE, SHAKE

He felt a sense of exhilaration as he entered Louisville's Central Station. It was 4:00 a.m., two hours before his non-stop train to New York City was scheduled to depart. The lobby was nearly deserted. A derelict, covered with newspapers, was curled on a bench. He was sleeping off a bottle or two of Sneaky Pete that lay at his feet. Two porters mopped away at a dull gray, lobby floor.

The captain positioned himself behind a post that gave him a clear view of the entrance yet offered some concealment. Two minutes passed, then three. Nothing.

He was sure he would be followed but was certain he had eluded anyone by having Frank Marconi pick up his automobile shortly after 3:00 a.m. and drive it to the city's other railroad station. Marconi was to wait at the station for 10 minutes, then drive back to the fort. Manigrove, meanwhile, had arranged for a taxi to pick him up at 3:30 a.m. and take him to Central Station, where he waited.

Sure, that he was clear of spying eyes, he moved swiftly to a bank of green, metal storage lockers located toward the rear of the lobby. He pulled out the package containing the $100,000 from beneath his jacket, placed it in locker 333, closed its door, deposited a quarter, turned the locker's key and then removed it. The money safely stored away, he took the key, placed it in a pre-addressed, stamped envelope, licked it closed and dropped it in a nearby mailbox. The envelope's glue left him with a sour taste.

The ticket windows had now opened, and a group of teenagers surged noisily into the lobby, followed by their high school teachers and chaperones. It reminded Manigrove of a cattle stampede he had once seen in a movie. Then he spotted the man, the same small, slim built man Lieutenant Fortunato had introduced him to at *The Twelve Angry Men*. It was Anthony Villano.

As Manigrove moved toward the ticket window, Villano moved to intercept him. Manigrove thought about running but to do so would be an admission of some kind of guilt. Better to bluff it out. He had a contingency plan.

"Let me see the money," Tony "Hits" said as he approached.

"I don't know what you are talking about," the captain responded.

"You know damn well what I'm talking about. I've got a .38 in my jacket, and it's aimed at your gut," "Hits" snarled.

"I am here at the station preparing for my journey to your wonderful City of New York. Why would I not have the package with me?" Manigrove asked.

"Because you set us up, you scum bag, so you could give us the slip," Tony answered. "You had us chasing some moron who had no idea why you had him drive your car to Union Station."

"That was a precautionary measure," Manigrove responded. "Since I was carrying a substantial amount of cash with me, I decided on a diversionary tactic to avoid robbery."

"If that's true, you got no trouble showing me the package now," said Tony.

"Well, of course not," the captain replied. With that, he pulled an identical package to the original from beneath his jacket.

Tony "Hits" scrutinized the package. Then said, "You bag of Southern shit. It doesn't have our mark on it. You pulled a switch, you fuck. Where's the real package?"

Manigrove realized he had been caught. But perhaps another bluff might buy him enough freedom to make a run for it. He smiled a weak smile at Tony "Hits" and said, "Just another diversionary tactic in case of robbers, Mr. Villano. Come. I will take you to where I hid the real package until train time." With that, he turned on his heel and headed toward the Men's Room.

As he entered the Men's Room, Tony was close behind. Manigrove entered a stall, whirled suddenly and smashed its door into "Hits"' face. Tony "Hits" staggered backward. Manigrove kicked him in the groin and landed a chop to the back of his neck. Tony made a hissing sound and fell to the tile floor. Manigrove raced out of the Men's Room, passed a gaggle of shocked teenagers and through a lobby exit door, where he was struck by something very hard. Franz Ludaniczech wiped the blood from the tire iron on the back of Manigrove's trench coat.

When he awoke, Manigrove found it difficult to open his left eye. It took him a moment to realize it had been glued shut by congealed blood that had run from his head wound. His head hurt very much, but he soon realized he was strapped into a metal chair that was clamped firmly to an oddly shaped steel pole. His feet rested on a circular metal platform that stood three feet above a concrete floor.

"Welcome to the shaking machine, Captain," said Carmela Fortunato.

Through the pain, Manigrove managed, "I do believe it is the lovely lieutenant who runs most things around this place."

"Yes, it is, and you will see how efficiently I run things." She paused. "Now listen to me carefully, Captain. If you tell us where the money is, we just might let bygones be bygones and let you go. If you choose to be difficult, we will force the truth out of you. Now, which shall it be?" Carmela asked.

Manigrove realized that no matter what he said, he would never leave this room alive. He sighed. "Madam, I can abide all kinds of theft and illegality, but what my family and I cannot abide is treason. And you are committing treason by using our people to give the Soviets a technological advantage. The Manigroves are Americans, first and last. Your Mafia family is betraying the land that gives it sustenance, a place to be, a place to operate from under laws that protect you. No profit can justify such betrayal. I threw the money down a sewer. There can be no profit in betraying us to the Russians."

Carmela gave one of her cute, enchanting little laughs. "Bullshit," she said. "You would no more throw that money away than cut off an arm. As for the patriotism crap, the United States and the Soviet Union are two competing mobs fighting over turf. Each is so big, it cannot knock off the other or put out a hit directly on the other. So, each gets allies to fight their little turf wars. Each has to cut deals, and that lets us little guys make a buck or two. But you, Captain, are not a patriot. You are a damn crook who tried to steal a lot of money from us. Now tell us where you put it. So, maybe we won't have to kill you."

"I must admit that I decided to turn a bad deed into a bit of family profit for the Manigroves. So for multiple reasons, I cannot tell you where the money is," he replied.

Tony brought a hammer down on the captain's fingers. Manigrove screamed but said nothing. Tony smashed the fingers of the other hand. Manigrove screamed again, and tears ran from his eyes. Suddenly, the pain in his hands was joined with a searing pain as Ludaniczech pressed a lit cigar against his neck. Manigrove's body flexed in agony, and he screamed again. The big guard pressed the cigar into the captain's flesh again. This time Manigrove just quivered. He was beyond such pain.

"Talk," Carmela commanded.

Manigrove just shook his head.

"Then, let's shake, rattle and roll," she replied and threw a switch.

It was a familiar sensation. Manigrove felt like he was traveling down a bumpy road, one with lots of ruts and very little pavement. He moved up and down, backward and forward and side to side. "Tolerable," he thought after the first five minutes. After ten, he was beginning to feel slight nausea. After 15 minutes, he noticed a slight speed up in the action. The entire platform began to move as well. Things whirled before his eyes.

This was like some terrible amusement park ride. Then suddenly, the machine stopped. Only his body seemed to keep spinning carrying his pain along. He remembered those days as a boy, when he and his friends would turn themselves round and round making themselves dizzy, finally falling to the ground and grasping it only to find that it swayed. They would laugh, knowing that soon the ground would be still. Now there was no ground, just stillness.

He opened his eyes and noticed a little blood had begun to trickle from the cut over his eye. The nausea faded. Then came Carmela's voice.

"Ready to tell me where the money is?"

"Sadly, no," Manigrove responded.

The machine started up again. This time, it ran for what seemed an eternity to Manigrove. The nausea had returned in all its retching ugliness. He could no longer contain himself. He began to vomit. The spin of the platform shot his spewing across his face. Blood was pooling in both his eyes, then flying off to somewhere in space.

Suddenly, he felt his body going the opposite way. The direction had been reversed. "No, it wasn't that because the up and down and back and forth motions had stopped. The machine had stopped. Then the voice came again.

"Tell me where the money is, Captain. This is a lousy way to die."

Manigrove's head slumped oddly to one side. The thought of moving made the illness grow stronger. He managed to muster only, "No."

"Damn son-of-a-bitch!" Carmela screamed as she threw the switch again.

Again, the spinning, the lurching, the bouncing up and up and down began. Only this time it was faster and unending. He knew she was going to kill him. Everything was flying in different directions. Manigrove began to vomit again. His stomach ached. Then his muscles went slack. Something snapped in his brain. He saw only red, then blackness, then nothing. Then death.

Tony "Hits" cleaned up Manigrove's body, and with the help of Franz Ludaniczech loaded the captain into the back of a stolen army truck. They drove out of the compound and down the Dixie Highway about half way to Louisville. They stopped, turned out the lights and got out. Tony grabbed Manigrove's legs; Ludaniczech caught the body under the arms.

"He feels like jelly," the big guard said.

"Just dump him in front of the truck," Tony "Hits" responded.

They laid him out arms spread, legs crossed. They climbed back into the truck and drove over the body. Contact made a slight bump. Tony put the vehicle in reverse and backed over the crushed form. This time there was no bump.

30

THE KILLING ROOM

Carmela marched Joey along a corridor lit by deep red bulbs.

"Open the door on your left and step in," Carmela ordered.

From the sound of her voice, Joey estimated that she was staying just out of reach in the event he suddenly turned. Best to go along, he thought, and wait for the opportunity, should she offer him one.

As he entered the room, Carmela, still behind him, flipped a switch and a bright, white light went on. It revealed a thickly padded room. "Soundproof," she said. "I could shoot you here, and Tony and Victor wouldn't hear a thing," she said.

"How about kissing me instead," Joey countered.

Lieutenant Gorgeous laughed. "You are cute but not that cute. I can't let pleasure interfere with business," she said. "How come a smart, educated guy like you wanted to stay in the army and become a cop?" she suddenly asked. "You could make all kinds of money outside. Why stay here?

"You've done your homework," he said.

"Thank Lieutenant Colonel Doyle and Tony," she answered. "It's always best to know your enemy, but you are a puzzle. A draftee, a couple of degrees. You fought like a crazed animal and saved somebody you barely knew. Why?"

"Freud, read Freud, read Jung," Joey answered. "I loved my mother, felt overwhelmed by my father, who I subconsciously wanted to kill, and turned my sexual desire into a striving for power. Beyond all that, I wanted adventure. The army offered me the opportunity to get all that."

"I might have really liked you," Carmela said. "It's too bad it has to end this way." She pointed the pistol at his heart, then said, "Not yet. You deserve to see this place. You will understand it. This room," she explained, "was built to test the extent to which loud noise can cause permanent loss of hearing. Animals and human volunteers sit in here for varying amounts of time where they are subjected to louder and louder noise. Mostly the sound simulates that of 155-millimeter cannons going off. It hurts," she said sounding as if she had tried the experience. "Many of our men returned from Korea with hearing loss," she continued. The army wants to know how to protect them better," she said. "Did you lose hearing, Master Sergeant?"

"I think so," Joey responded. "Sometimes I have a ringing in my head."

"Interesting," she said. "Tony complains of the same thing. Now come." She motioned toward the door. She ordered him to turn left down the red-lit corridor. They walked 20 steps and came to a large glass panel. Carmela flipped a switch revealing what looked like an operating room. "This is not an ordinary operating room. See those vents there, near the ceiling and the floor?" Joey nodded.

In this room, volunteers are strapped down naked on the table. Thermocouples are placed in their various orifices to send temperature signals to this panel. "The 'patients,'" she said with a laugh, "are then boiled or frozen at different humidities. They must respond to questions until they become delirious or unconscious. Then the doctors try to revive them. It's a new thing for the doctors. They are learning."

"Lots of our guys froze along the Yalu River," Joey said.

"The Germans had similar problems with their pilots who were shot down over the English Channel in winter and of course with their soldiers in Russia," Carmela responded. "But, they, as usual, were very efficient. As their men froze, their medical corps filmed the efforts to save them. Our experts now study seized German Army films to learn from them. I understand that one of their techniques was to place the frozen man between two naked women who would attempt to stimulate him. Interesting, huh?"

"And what was the result?" Joey asked.

"Inconclusive," Lieutenant Gorgeous replied with a smile. "You've seen enough. Now to the shaking room, where Tony and Victor await us," she said, suddenly looking very ugly.

Carmela pointed Joey back down the red-lit corridor, then down a flight of stairs to a large gray door. She pressed a button, and the door opened revealing a room about as big as an airplane hangar. The walls and floor were as gray as the door. At the center, lay a huge wheel, perhaps 20 feet in diameter. Its hub was a hydraulic piston. It could have been a lift auto mechanics use when working beneath a car, except it was shorter and had a huge amount of play. It also had a chair welded to the piston two feet above the wheel.

"What in the hell is that for?" Joey asked as he entered the room.

"It has no official name. But we call it the Shaking Machine," answered Gorgeous. "The 8-8-5-2 built it right here to solve a little military problem. The army bought $20 million worth of newly designed personnel carriers, and immediately put them out in the field. The carriers worked great. They easily moved over the roughest terrain. They even motor-boated across rivers. But when the soldiers came out, some had trouble standing; some fell; many vomited. None of them could fight. So, the big shots gave us the problem and said, 'How do we fix it?'"

Colonel Doyle had this machine built to simulate the motion of the personnel carrier. It goes up and down, tilts and wobbles at the same time. It's like a very nasty amusement park ride, not really fun. We strapped a monkey into the chair and duplicated the motion of the personnel carrier. After 24 hours of shaking, the monkey was dead. We cut him open and found that the nerve endings around his spine had come apart. We repeated the experiment a couple of times, and always got the same result. The assholes had built a carrier that literally was shaking its personnel to death. Imagine paying $20 million for that. They should have sold it to the Chinese."

"Did this machine kill Manigrove?" Joey asked.

"What the hell," Lieutenant Gorgeous answered, "Considering that you will take this to your grave . . . Yes. It shook him to death."

"Was he about to reveal that Doyle was a traitor?" Joey pressed.

Carmela laughed. "No. The idiot had no idea what Doyle was doing. He died because he cheated my family and embarrassed me. We had made him a deal. He wanted money; we gave it to him. He was our money courier. He moved our money from the sales of the televisions and hi-fi radios without a problem. As an officer investigating this place, he gave us perfect cover. No one questioned his coming and going. It worked nicely until he got greedy. When the pot suddenly got bigger, he decided to steal the pot. And I thought you could trust Southern gentlemen. He was supposed to deliver $100,000 we had gotten from the Russians and deliver it to the Lanteri family in New York. Instead, he stole it."

"One hundred thousand dollars from the Russians? What for?" Joey asked.

"They need American expertise to solve a computer problem, something to do with a space shot they are planning. They asked us to supply the experts for $100,000 a month plus expenses. We told them to put the money up front, and they did. Those kid scientists jumped on the project like it was a great big game. Of course, they think they're working for Uncle Sam, so we don't have to pay them. A beautiful setup. But somehow, Manigrove found out and decided the patriotic thing to do was steal our money. We caught up with him at the railroad station. We used the shaking machine to make him tell us where he hid the cash."

"And he didn't tell," Joey said.

"But, maybe you will," Gorgeous answered. "If you can tell us where the money is, you just might leave here alive."

"I don't know where the money is, but if I did, I wouldn't tell you anyway," Joey snapped back. "I'm going to end up like Captain Manigrove no matter what I say—dead and dumped on the side of the road," answered Joey.

"You bet your ass," snarled Victor Rodney. He, Tony "Hits" and Franz Ludaniczech had been standing next to the controls of the shaking machine, listening. Tony and the guard were deadpan.

"Put him on," Carmela ordered.

Rodney moved quickly behind Joey and struck him hard in the back with the butt of his pistol. "That's for the beating you gave me!" he yelled. Joey staggered forward then dropped to one knee and with a single motion pulled out the pistol strapped to his ankle. He heard the hammer on Rodney's weapon click back. Then a shot rang out. Rodney toppled on Joey, blood pouring from his mouth. Tony "Hits" had put a bullet between his eyes.

"You bastard!" Gorgeous screamed as she fired her pistol at Tony. Tony stood staring at her, his snub-nosed revolver pointing at her chest. Then he fell backward a large hole in his heart. Joey thought he saw a flash of disbelief in Tony's dying eyes. He didn't have time to think about that now. He fired and hit a charging Ludaniczech in the throat. He knew he was late as he spun toward Carmela. The next shot would be hers. But it wasn't. Instead, it came from the doorway of the shaking room. The bullet caught her in the face. Her body struck the wall behind her then slid to the floor, leaving a splash of blood in its wake. She wasn't gorgeous anymore. She was ugly and dead.

Joey turned toward the figure at the door. It was Special Agent Mark Laurens. His .45 caliber was still aimed at the spot in which Carmela had stood. "I saw that fella grab you, and I followed," he said.

"Thanks," Joey managed.

"No, thank you," Laurens replied. "You led me to these bastards. And I got to hear that Captain Albert Ruppert Manigrove III was not a traitor."

"Just a thief," answered Joey.

"Just a man trying to do the best by his family. You know sending profits back to the family is a Manigrove tradition. It is a responsibility that every Manigrove carries with him throughout his life. Profit is the family's motivator, second only to patriotism. A man can make his money wisely or badly, as long as he makes it. But he can never, never be a traitor. The Manigroves have always been thankful that this land gave them opportunity. They shed blood from Revolutionary days to uphold that freedom." Laurens smiled. "I guess I never told you. Captain Manigrove was my cousin. No accident I was on this case. The Manigroves have a certain influence at the upper levels of the Justice Department."

Joey shook his head in disbelief.

"Don't be upset," Laurens said. "We got the spies. We got the crooks. You're alive. I found out the truth. I'd say we all had a pretty good day."

"Yeah," Joey replied. "I guess we better get the general to clean up this mess."

As they walked out of the shaking room together, Laurens put his hand in his pocket and fingered the key to locker 333 at the Central Train Station. He knew now why Cousin Albert had mailed it to the clan. It was money the Manigroves could honestly take.

31

EPILOGUE
IN THE HOUSE OF GOD

Joey arrived back at his motel room, removed his torn and blood-spattered sports jacket and flopped into a stuffed, slightly uncomfortable easy chair. He opened a small bottle of Jack Daniels and poured himself a shot over a glass of ice. It was time to put all the pieces together. The spies had been caught, the mob broken up, all without damaging Shorty Stockton's career.

But Tony was dead. He grieved over Tony Villano. It was as if God had played a mischievous game with them for some celestial amusement. Joey had saved Tony's life nearly at the price of his own at the Han River. Now Tony had given his life to save Joey. Maybe Tony was doomed to die young and violently. Maybe God had saved him just so he could save Joey. When he had done that, God took him back. If Gorgeous hadn't shot him, Laurens certainly would have. Or maybe living and dying was all just so much chance. And maybe there is no God, and maybe if there is he, she, it, doesn't give a damn about the

Tony's and Joey's who happen along and are gone in a blink anyway. Joey sipped the Jack, which felt warm and comforting as it went down.

Then there was Laurens, the cold bastard, listening patiently outside the shaking room so he could find out whether Manigrove was a plain crook or a patriotic crook. The Manigroves were as much members of a mob family as Tony was.

Finally, there was Doyle, once a patriot, then a spy and perhaps, in the end, some kind of Jesus or Don Quixote or both trying to save the world from itself. And that led to the one loose end. Wade or Walensky or whoever he was. He had disappeared, gone AWOL. The MPs had searched the fort. They had searched Louisville with the help of Detective Mike Theiss, but Wade was nowhere to be found.

Then the phone rang.

"Sergeant Klugman?" the accented voice asked.

"Yes," Joey replied into its food speckled speaker.

"Be at Temple Beth Shalom services tomorrow night." With that, the caller hung up.

The Beth Shalom Temple is in the older part of Louisville. But it is neither historic nor of particular beauty. It is a storefront shul used by a declining orthodox community that makes up with fervor what it lacks in numbers. Joey had attended an orthodox shul during his formative years because his non-practicing father wanted to please his pious wife. Joey's maternal grandfather, a man with an overpowering beard of pure white and suits of deep black, had orchestrated the family's religious practices as long as Joey could remember. They had prayed at the shul, and they had prayed at home. They had eaten only kosher foods always from the appropriate plates. Grandpa died after Joey's bar mitzvah, and it was over. Joey, like his father, became non-practicing.

But occasionally, Joey's dad would take him back to the old shul, a storefront similar to Beth Shalom in Louisville. They would wait outside until the truly devout had entered and then seat themselves at the very back. Joey would follow the scriptures and pronounce the Hebrew words without understanding them. His father would simply mumble prayers, rise, genuflect and sit at the appropriate times. Then, one day, as they walked home, Joey got the courage to ask his father: "Pop, why do we come here? I don't really pray, and you just make sounds."

"I ask myself that question also. I have no answer. No rational answer anyway," his father said. "All I can say is that I feel at home here. There is something about the hum and the chants of the prayers. The sing-song. The hard benches. The taluses. The worn, old prayer books. Even the shabby Torahs. They pull me back here, not really to pray, just to feel and touch and move and smell. Yes, a shul has a smell. It is part pious sweat, part decaying prayer books, and part I can't explain. Maybe it smells of God. Coming back here is touching my roots."

"What if there is no God, then those men are bending and swaying and praying to nothing at all?" Joey pressed on, angry, though he didn't know why.

"It doesn't matter," his father answered. "If God is there, that's fine. And if he isn't, that's fine too. What matters is that we are here, and they are here, and we find our strength in each other, that we hold a common belief and show it in our own peculiar way." Then he smiled. "And the orthodox are the most peculiar of our people. The others, the Conservative, the Reform, they make rational, understandable compromises with time and place. The people in there make no compromises. For them, truth can never change even if it defies what their eyes tell them. So, we visit them. We draw strength from them, but we cannot stay with them because we know that there is truth as well in what we see."

Joey returned to his religion in a large auditorium at Camp Kilmer, New Jersey, just a few days after being drafted. An enormous sergeant stood on a large stage looking out at a thousand seated recruits, and with a voice that needed no amplification, he bellowed, "Protestants get up and stand in the aisle to your left; Catholics to the aisle on your right. And Jews get in the back. And I don't want to see anyone sitting." Joey sprinted to the back of the auditorium.

Now, as he sat on the hard-cushioned pew in Beth Shalom mouthing Hebrew and watching a few old men pray, he thought about his father—a nice man who only wanted peace and twice found war, first his own, then his son's.

"Master Sergeant Joseph Klugman," the accented voice said from just behind him. "My name is Jeffrey Wade."

Joey turned and looked into the eyes of a tall, slender young man. He was better looking than the photograph he had seen of him in his personnel file. Then, almost everyone was.

"You are Gregor Walensky. You have been AWOL for the past week."

"And under suspicion of being a spy," Wade finished the sentence. "For now, I am Wade. Soon enough, I will be Walensky."

"Why are you here? In this temple? You know I am going to arrest you."

Wade rose and moved into Joey's pew, sitting beside him. "I have taken a risk to meet with you. I have told the two KGB outside that I wanted to pray one more time here before leaving this country. I would not leave willingly with them if they did not let me. Before I got to America, I barely knew I was a Jew, only that I was being persecuted for being one. Since being here, I have done some reading and attended some services in this very shul. Frankly, I find much of the ritual anachronistic—the wrapping of the phylacteries, the bending and swaying, the constant thanking of God, the constant bemoaning of our fate as a sign that God is punishing us for failing to live up to our commitments to him. And our unending optimism . . . incredible."

Joey looked at Wade incredulously. "You brought me here to discuss your Jewishness? I guess you just don't get it. I don't care if you are a direct descendant of Moses. I'm placing you under arrest." Joey stood, groping for the handcuffs he carried on his belt.

Several of the elderly men stopped their davening to stare at them.

"Wait," Jeffrey Wade implored, putting a hand on Joey's sleeve. "I have something to trade."

"What?"

"My father."

Joey let his hand drop from his belt. "Your father?"

"Yes. I assume you know he is one of the world's leading physicists and that he is working for your government at one of your prestigious universities."

"I read your dossier," Joey responded.

"Soviet agents recently learned where my father is living. As we speak, they are preparing to spirit him out of your country. I do not think that would be good for world peace. He is on the verge of breakthroughs that will lead to exponential growth in our use of nuclear energy and potentially the development of unbelievably powerful explosives, dwarfing the hydrogen bomb."

"Fine," said Joey. "I will alert the CIA and the FBI, and they will cordon him off."

"Too late," Jeffrey Wade replied. "The Soviets already have him. I know where, and I will give you the location if you let me walk out of here free. The KGB will slip me out of the United States. I am to join my father in the Soviet Union where we will work together to expand the Kremlin's power. With the greatest modesty, I would say putting my father and me at the disposal of those men puts the world at enormous risk. Having one of us in each camp neutralizes the situation. So, I make a trade. I go with the KGB. You keep my father. We will balance each other out."

"Each of you would balance the other's capacity to terrorize mankind," Joey said. "Something like Solomon offering to slice the baby in half, a solution that satisfies neither."

"Precisely. It is a devil's bargain, but it is a bargain, a Walensky standoff," Jeffrey replied.

"I am not the man to make that decision," Joey answered.

"You are the only man in a position to make that decision," Wade replied. "If I do not walk out that door in the next five minutes, those agents will come in. Would you have a shoot-out in here?"

Joey sat down and looked up at the ceiling. "Why me, Oh, Lord," he thought.

"I have read that 'Tikkun olam' is a fundamental Hebrew phrase meaning Jews have an obligation to repair the world," Wade said.

"Through commitment to God," Joey answered. "Letting two scientific terrorists go at each other is not what I would call showing a commitment to God."

"But it is," Wade replied. "As presented to us, God's law is divided into two parts, first our commitment to this one great entity, second our commitment to each other. 'Do onto others as you would have them do onto you.' It is that part of the commitment we face right now, right here."

Joey thought for a long moment. He shivered. It was suddenly cold in this house of God. "Tell me where your father is being held, and I will let you go free," Joey said.

"There is a small house near the Soviet estate in Glen Cove, New York. They have taken him there. They intend to take him out tonight and place him on an Aeroflot jet headed for Moscow. That is all I know," said Wade.

He got up quickly, patted Joey on the shoulder and moved to the door.

Joey stood up behind him, pulled out his pistol and aimed it at Wade's back. "Stop, or I will shoot you," he said.

Wade shrugged, opened the door and began to walk away.

THE END

Made in the USA
Columbia, SC
31 October 2021